PLAYING WITH
MISCHIEF

H.A. Willis

MMXXI

Playing with Mischief

First published in Australia by H.A. Willis 2021

 A catalogue record for this
book is available from the
National Library of Australia

ISBN: 978-0-6451884-2-4 (pbk)
ISBN: 978-0-6451884-3-1 (ebk)

Cover image H.A. Willis © 2021

Typesetting and design by Publicious Book Publishing
Published in collaboration with Publicious Book Publishing
www.publicious.com.au

For Mum & Dad

Liar, liar, pants on fire!
— Schoolyard taunt

"Devilment is the nicest thing in life."
— Robert Walser.

Invocation

One warm, inland day Henry Morgan received the telegram notifying him of his elevation to District Inspector. The following morning a shining, registered letter arrived from Head Office. Signed by the Commissioner of Crown Lands, it confirmed Morgan's promotion and directed him to report to Caywood District Office on the first Monday of the new year. The incumbent Caywood Inspector would remain for a week to provide the necessary official and social introductions; to familiarize Morgan with all outstanding business and to show him around his District. On the 12th of January, the new Inspector's posting being advertised in that week's *Government Gazette*, the handover would become official. After requesting Morgan to confirm a reservation at the boarding house selected to serve as his accommodation until the Department's house was vacated by the present occupant, the Commissioner took the opportunity of personally wishing his Inspector every success in his new position.

Morgan softly rubbed the top right corner of the Commissioner's letter between his thumb and forefinger. The foolscap sheet was of a weight and texture he had not seen since before the war. The blue ink from the Commissioner's fountain pen carried a slight iridescence, a vivid sheen that gave the impression it had only just dried. Although familiar with the bold signature from its printed reproduction at the foot of official notices and proclamations, Morgan felt the larger original directly imparted confidence and quiet authority to him — to him, specifically. It was as if the man himself had stood before Morgan, looked him in the eye, shook his hand and patted him on the shoulder. The document he held in his hand was a warrant of substance, a letters patent admitting Morgan into a fraternity; a welcoming salutation as a member of that select band of men charged with marching across broad acres and negotiating barbed wire fences in order to stand astride windy rises and heft their binoculars in search of vermin, noxious weeds, soil erosion or any other violation of designated land use.

Above all, Morgan was gratified to be granted stewardship of a District as large and, it was generally acknowledged, as challenging as Caywood. Those who watched such things, those in the know, appreciated that such an appointment was not lightly bestowed upon a newly promoted Inspector. It was an indication the powers-that-be considered their appointee to be a man with a clear and bright future in the Lands Department. Morgan's friends and colleagues around the State understood this sign of favour and used the occasion of the festive season to congratulate him.

As pleasing and flattering as such associative expressions of goodwill certainly were, the extra cards her husband unexpectedly received in the last days before Christmas left Dolly flummoxed, perhaps even a little vexed, because their late arrival left insufficient time for her to exercise the courtesy of reply by return post.

It was, as she wrote to her mother and married sisters, all a bit rushed. The Department's transfer allowance covered the expenses of moving their goods and chattels the 120 miles south from Betagulla to

Caywood, but Morgan and Dolly had to see to the arrangements and do the packing themselves. It all had to be wrapped and packed into tea chests and much of that wearisome work necessarily fell to Dolly. She soldiered on without complaint and Morgan once again quietly congratulated himself on having married such an amenable and practical woman.

It was commonly remarked that Dolly was a real asset to Morgan. She had a comely figure but dressed decorously. A good dancer, she could carry her side in conversational niceties without imbibing more than a social shandy on a hot day. If there was one thing it was that, regardless of her sunny common sense, she remained a farm girl without the polish or schooling to hide her feelings when it may have been prudent to do so. Without quite putting it into words in his own mind, Morgan sensed that his wife's innocent candour could leave her vulnerable in the urbane but sometimes competitive social atmosphere associated with a large Regional Office. In the country towns where Morgan expected his career to initially flourish, however, Dolly's common touch was more likely to assist his progress.

All and sundry nodded easy agreement that a good wife was essential to a man's advancement. But in Morgan's case those in the know, those with their ears to the ground, also heard the breath of a whisper from the quiet, inner chambers of Head Office. There, someone let it be known, Morgan's greatest asset was seen as his aptitude for paperwork. Slapdash paperwork, it was said, was the Achilles' heel of many an otherwise able field officer. It was an open secret Morgan "carried" the Betagulla Inspector, a bereaved man who had taken to the drink. Morgan's silent loyalty to his superior was noticed and appreciated. His orderly intelligence not only got things done, it got them done right first time. Should, for example, a landholder persistently defy the Department's remit, Morgan could be relied upon to assemble such sworn evidence that no Stipendiary Magistrate would hesitate to convict the summonsed offender.

Morgan took Dolly home for Christmas. They set out from Betagulla in the afternoon for the seven-hour drive to her parents' dairy farm in the State's south-east. Their only stop was for petrol on the outskirts of the Capital. There, in the Christmas Eve twilight, as they ate their corned beef sandwiches and had a cup of tea, it started to rain. Morgan had new tyres and a good spare so they pushed on and the reliable old Dodge Tourer ran sweet and even in the unseasonably cool weather. Being Christmas Eve there was, of course, some other traffic on the roads, but not as much as Morgan had expected and as they passed through the succession of small towns to the east and the night wore on they had fewer and fewer bright headlights coming at them. The meticulously maintained car's wipers ticked away like a metronome but Morgan remained alert. When they finally turned off the highway they had the narrow back road to themselves. Everybody was waiting for them and the men, after unpacking the car, took a whiskey or two before the open fire.

On Boxing Day, the Capital's newspapers reported the novelty of a White Christmas in the mountains to the north of Dolly's people's place. They saw no snow, but Dolly's father, born and raised in the locality, swore he had never experienced such a cold, wet Christmas. Things were out of kilter, said the breeder of Jersey cattle. He shook his head and said his father, who had cleared the land in the days of the Colony, would never have believed such weather possible.

After five days at his in-laws, Morgan took Dolly to

spend a few days over the New Year with his parents in their seaside town two hours' drive further east. Morgan and his father, a retired High School teacher, went fishing. Dolly and her mother-in-law baked a sponge cake and exchanged a few tame confidences. She and Morgan were, she assured his mother, "trying". They agreed, it was only a matter of time.

Dolly was then returned to her family and early one morning Morgan kissed her lips and left to make the long drive back to and through the Capital and out towards the western plains.

On a low ridge at the eastern edge of his District, Morgan pulled over to pour himself his last mug of Thermos tea. He got out of the car to stretch his legs. Under scattered clouds gliding before the southerly, he contemplated the patchwork of light and shade moving over the serene face of the land. Letting his gaze drift from the dark hills in the south to the bright plains in the north, he looked upon the Domain with which he had been entrusted and found it truly pleasing to behold.

A fortnight later, having taken possession of and installed his furniture in the Departmental house, he returned to the city to be waiting on the platform as Dolly's train steamed in from the east. In a clean summer shirt and a stylish new hat, he stood with his legs apart, hands in pockets, a picture of casual confidence. That night, after treating themselves to a flash meal and a Technicolor film, they stayed in a comfortable hotel. Dolly also enjoyed the arm-in-arm window-shopping stroll around the city with her easygoing husband.

Mild weather had held until mid-January, but that Saturday the real season was suddenly made manifest by a strong, parching northerly. It blew all day under a shimmering glare and the temperature rose to nudge the century. That night, Morgan left their fifth-floor room window open to catch any breeze off the bay. At around half past four in the morning he woke to the pale smell of distant smoke. He went to the window, saw the breeze had shifted to the west and understood that somewhere out there in the wild gullies and along the sharp ridges of the coastal ranges a bushfire had gotten away. It may even have been in a State Forest in the southern part of his District. A fire in such inaccessible country could only be left to burn itself out. He drank a glass of water, closed the window, lowered the blind and calmly went back to bed with his sleeping wife.

Parking the car under a shady tree and then wandering around the Botanical Gardens, they waited in the city until the forecast cool change brought relief after lunch. For the drive to Caywood Dolly tied her hair back and wound down the window. The road noise and wind subdued conversation, but it was pleasant travelling alone together. Late in the afternoon Morgan stopped at the vantage point to show his young wife the vista of his realm. A veil of diffused smoke remained high in the sky. He pointed to a distant copper gleam and named a lake. At the southern end, he told her, was Caywood. He handed her his binoculars but the town was lost in the haze and lowering sun.

Within an hour of opening his Office Monday morning, Morgan was hearing rumours of the fire having been deliberately lit. It was said there were at least three starting points along a disused logging track running beside a State Forest to the south-west of Caywood. Someone on horseback, it was speculated, had ridden across country and along the bush track. The blaze had been contained by a cool change and light showers coming over from the coast, but a thousand smoking trees and logs lay in wait for the hot winds forecast for the weekend. Morgan was kept busy that week by meetings with Shire officials, Fire and Police officers. He and his Assistant spent several days visiting the numerous farms from which an arsonist may have gained access to the supposed seats of the fire. Morgan did not need his Assistant, a local boy, to see that none of the farmers they spoke to would have ever had anything to do with lighting fires. They could all vouch for their few employees and none of them had actually seen the elusive horseman, who by mid-week had become a fixture in city newspaper reports. The Inspector from the neighbouring district telephoned to report he and the local police had no suspects. It was a mystery.

On that same Monday morning a couple of women with toddlers in tow had yoo-hooed at Dolly's front door and introduced themselves. Over a quick cup of tea and a cigarette Dolly sized up her neighbours, wives of other public servants, and accepted their invitations for return visits. The women offered to help unpack the tea chests, but Dolly politely said she and Morgan preferred to sort things out themselves. As her guests were leaving one of them slowed in the hallway to glance into the bedroom. The woman waivered on the threshold, seemingly about to say something; but her companion, declaring the morning was getting away from them, took her elbow and briskly led her out of the house. Returning from closing the front door, Dolly paused to examine the view of the bedroom from the hallway. Satisfied with the pillow fold of the crisp sheets and the even fall line of the bedspread on the neatly made bed, she ran her eyes over the few items on her dressing table. In doing so she noticed, reflected in one of the wing mirrors, the door of the wardrobe was ajar with the tie rack extended. At the fore was the bright purple Donald Duck item Morgan won in Luna Park the previous summer. "No secrets in a country town," Dolly told herself, and went back to her interrupted work.

At the end of the week a capricious north-westerly got around to nuzzling and licking all those smouldering logs. Sparks flew and found places to land. The fire stood up, stretched its wings and took off along the ridges. It pounced on a small sawmill and half a dozen of its workers' cottages. Everybody got out in time, although in some cases with just the clothes they stood in. Three or four dairy farmers had a worrisome few days and nights, but no stock was lost and only a few fences were destroyed. The fire remained in the hills, where it spent another week rummaging through the remotest tracts of forest throwing up a vast, spreading plume of smoke.

And ash.

One night the wind switched and was sucked up into a high corner of the dark sky. Just before dawn it exhaled and, with all the dogs barking and howling, the town woke in a lurid orange glow. A black snow of perfectly carbonized leaves fell on Caywood. There were no embers, only crisply curled eucalyptus leaves. They fell through the muted air, drifting down, twisting like unholy tadpoles, skittering in the streets, whispering on the rooves and piling up in the gutters.

The scorched reek furled into Morgan's dreams. He woke in fright and rushed out onto the front lawn in his pyjamas. He felt the leaves crunch to ash beneath his bare feet. Retreating to the veranda, he wiped his blackened soles and went inside to fetch his slippers, dressing gown and camera. Knowing the monochrome film would only capture the light as a grey murk, he looked about for a contrasting background. He called Dolly after him and had her stand on the front step in her dressing gown. She could see that the spectacle excited him, but she wrinkled her nose and refused to venture out beyond the cover of the eave. He photographed her there, looking fretfully at the amber sky, as, to her left, wafting as lightly as dandelion seeds, half a dozen leaves blurred down across the white weatherboard house front. Cautioning him to wipe his feet and shake off his dressing gown she went inside to light the stove before going back to wait for him in bed. He walked over to the front gate and looked up and down the empty street. The burnt leaves continued to fall.

Just as he was about to return to the house he heard a motor cranked to life somewhere down the western end of the street. Morgan guessed it was the greengrocer's old Chev. After a few coughing splutters it settled to a steady rattle. He heard the gears engage and as it shifted into third Morgan finally saw the truck solidify out of the gloom. The big antique headlights loomed as the yellow eyes of some rough beast and their beams picked out the swirling leaves precisely. Morgan took his photograph when the vehicle was about fifty yards away on the far side of the road. In years to come, in other times and places, the resulting ghostly image would be considered artistic, but on that morning the greengrocer merely gave the photographer a laconic salute as he passed.

Wiping his feet and shaking off his dressing gown, Morgan went back inside to add wood and stoke up the stove before joining his wife in their marriage bed. As he covered her, all in a rosy glow, she smelt and breathed in the smoke in his hair.

Mischief

As surely as that sooty K class now staunchly snorts up the steady mile incline from the wheat silos to Ponds Road, the day is coming when an automatic boom and flashing lights will replace the wiry little gatekeeper. He has ruled this crossing since the year the King died, when a shunting accident put him on a part-pension. But, thirteen years on, the Spirit of Progress has not yet rolled over him and in this chill twilight the brass insignia and visor of his black hat gleam as he once more complacently limps from the cottage where his sunny wife stirs the evening stew. He sizes up the snow front looming in the south-west and lights his ruby lamps, glances back down the line at the silver-grey column of smoke stacking above the approaching locomotive, lets through a last car (nods to the driver) as he kicks out the swivelled props and, with perfect judgment of their momentum, gathers himself to swing his beautifully maintained gates. At that very moment the big engine's whistle skirls on the winter air and a pubescent juvenile, the picture of lanky delinquency, careens his whizzing bicycle into the top end of Ponds Road and pedals like blazes to beat the gates.

He was never going to make it.

The gates drag their clattering stirrups across the rails and shudder shut while the youth is still at least fifty yards up the street. The keeper is back at the pedestrian gate brusquely banging home the bolt before the cavalier cyclist skids up and casually extends a long leg to prop himself on his flashy machine.

The old man eyes the butterfly handlebars, the electric-blue paintwork, the disconnected tail-light, the sloppy duffle-coat and the indolent streak himself — and feels a bounce of satisfaction. His snug pleasure expands as he flips open and snaps shut his pocket watch to assure himself that he, he for one, he will be in his armchair in time for the footy highlights televised from Melbourne while the lout behind him will be left to race the swiftly approaching darkness home.

Two hundred yards or so down the line the incline crests onto the flat stretch that runs through the crossing and straight on out of town. Getting into stride, the lumbering giant rolls through the crossing with driver and gatekeeper holding laconic salutes. The gleaming rails ring and sing, the creaking wagons trundle by (boy and man count thirty-eight) and the lights of the swaying guard's van slide out on a diminishing clickety-clack, clickety-clack, never comin' back, clickety-clack. Click, clack. A farewell whistle hollows and unfurls back along the train as it gathers speed for its night ride across the wind flat western plains.

Hurry home. Late for tea. Mum'll be niggly. Bugger that old devil and his gates. Now it really *is* dark. A great draft of sudden wind sweeps in to meet the boy. Down Ponds Road the dynamo whirrs and the grey road shines by the swishing, hissing darkness of the old oaks and firs in the park. Dead leaves skitter through the iron railing fence.

Somewhere in there, way away back at the far end of the lake, where the untendered oaks have flourished into medieval forest, is the haunt of Apple Jack. A tough old bastard who keeps to himself. Said to have been a POW of the Japanese, the authorities leave him alone. Lives in a hollow tree. A corrugated iron mia-mia. Or in the labyrinth of century old tunnels on Chinaman's Hill, beyond the park's southern boundary. Some say he has Vegemite jars of gold specks and dust buried deep in abandoned shafts known only to him, the rabbits and ghosts. Others will tell you he takes eels and ducks from the lake, possums and picnic scraps from the park, rabbits and rats from the rampant furze thickets of Chinaman's Hill. Wherever he is, he'll be cold tonight.

Where the road levels the bike's headlamp dims to insignificance as the rider puts his head into the wind and stands on the pedals to struggle past the cold lake and its black breath of dredge weed and drowned babies. There's only one streetlight down there on that stretch and it's an awful long push to the next one. The boy's coat billows on flooding air and an icy snout nuzzles his armpits.

Nunga Perkins says there's at least ten foot of mud oozing in the belly of the lake and that's why they never ever find the bodies of anyone drowned in there. No floaters in that lake. Mud sucks them down forever. Nunga reckons there's a hole out near the middle too deep to fathom. Just a bit towards the convent side. Nunga knows about the bottomless lake because he used to have an uncle who worked on the weed-cutting dredge. That was the uncle died of a heart attack barracking at the footy. Died happy, sez Nunga, Carlton was getting done like a dinner.

Hope they got done today. *Good old Collingwood forever. Good old ...* Christ, it's cold! Cold as a witch's tit.

Turn away from the lake and go up a bit to turn again into Crimea Street. Houses with lighted windows. Now with his back to the torrent of freezing air, his lamp blazes. Flying home past Rose's newsagency: Saturday night and the bright interior is crowded with working men hanging around for the late edition of The Sporting Globe. A moth flits over his shoulder into the beam of his light. And another ... snowflakes. Out onto the wrong side of the road to hurtle around his corner wide and fast. The streetlight outside his home softens to become the core of an incandescent nova ball of blizzard.

He comes in as the kids are scurrying from the steamy bathroom to the lounge room to dry their hair by the open fire. In the kitchen the kettle and pots are bee busy on the stove as Mum ladles pea and ham soup while also keeping an eye on great-Auntie Jo, who, glasses fogged, shoulders like a centre-half forward, is wildly whacking butter onto a teetering deck, a whole loaf of thick toast. Noise and warmth, lights on in every room, misted windows and drawn curtains, sister's sly smirk and Mum's flushed, angry face exclude and make the weather outside irrelevant.

"You! Roger!" Her finger is rigid with accusation. "You were distinctly told to be home by an hour ago. An *hour* ago! Where've you been? As if I haven't enough to worry about. You could've been knocked off your bike and be bleeding to death in a gutter for all I knew. Where've you been at this time of night? And don't give me any of your long-winded, convoluted fibs. I can see right through you, my boy."

"Fibs! I ... " Flustered indignation. Struck speechless by the injustice of it all.

"Come on." She steps forward, damp tea towel ready to swat.

"Me an' Mike. Me an' Mike was in his shed, like — just muckin' round an' then we fed the ferrets an' we was ... "

"*Ferrets!* Dirty, stinking, pink-eyed *cruel* things. You make sure you wash your hands properly before you sit at table in *this* house. Don't Michael Ryan's parents know you have to be home before dark?"

"Yeah! 'course they do. But, see, the ferrets, one got out and we had to corner it and ... "

"Lord save us! You're lucky the little brute didn't bite you."

"And ... kinda forgot the time. Honest!" He turns on the old nothing-to-hide look. Mum narrows her eyes in judgment, the balance ready to tip on a breath. "Then I got caught at the gates by a goods train. Cor! Talk about taking its time. I lost count. Honest! There'd be sixty, seventy trucks. At least! Took ages'n'ages."

"And who else was there?" A stubborn stain of suspicion on her voice.

"Who? Where? At Mike's?"

Her eyes warn him.

"Nobody else was there. We was, we was ... honest Mum! Just me an' Mike!"

"And Nunga Perkins," Janice simper sneers as she passes Auntie Jo the last slices of toast.

Mum is immediately back on the war path. "I've told you! I don't want you seeing that Perkins lout. I blame that damned cousin of yours — that bloody Larry got yous all in thick together and up to no good last summer. Perkins is too old for you. I never know what you're up to following him around. He wasn't expelled without reason. The sooner they put him in the army, the better. Keep away from him. D'ya hear me?"

"He wasn't there!"

"I mean it!"

"Haven't seen him!"

"If I find out otherwise, you won't be going near the Ryans' again. I hope Mrs Ryan has the sense to chase him off. You'd better look me in the eye and tell me he wasn't there."

"*Mum! He wasn't!* Geez! Never see him since he got 'is car." The rims of his ears burn as they thaw.

Hmmm.

"Honest." The bottom line.

Mum relaxes and glances at the stove. Something smells good. Wholesome good.

"Snowing outside," he says with his best guileless smile. "Heaps of it coming down. Oughta let the kids have a geek."

Auntie Jo suddenly squawks like a startled chook and Janice, buttered wodge of toast in hand, jumps clear of flailing hands, one of which holds a knife. A sharp knife.

"Janice! I told you not to upset her. I'll skin you alive, you bloody trouble-making little minx. Get out of here before you make me good'n'angry."

To the distant surf roar of a televised football crowd, Janice slips through the sliding door into the lounge room.

"Little minx." Mum returns to the soup and Auntie Jo subsides to desultory clucking as she rearranges her disturbed stack of toast.

"Your father had to get the wood in. Again! That's your job and you should be here to do it. And don't forget it. Now wash your hands — ferrets! — and ... Put the plate ... Auntie Jo, put the plate of toast on the table. Yes, that's right. On-the-table. God spare me days!"

He hesitates in the doorway, then ducks across to follow his sister into the lounge.

"Geez Dad." Bright and cheery. "Geez, sorry about the wood. Mike's ferret got out and we had to catch it. How's the footy going?"

One of the kids calls from behind the drapes. "Come look at the snow. Dad, come look, quick."

Dad's movement to rise from his chair is arrested by a brilliant mark taken by the Collingwood forward.

"Boy, what a beauty!" Roger enthuses, rapt attention. "Who's in front?"

"Bloke on the wireless reckoned this was the winning kick. Don't the Ryans listen to the footy?"

"Yeah! 'course. But me an' Mike was in the shed."

The little figure wobbles on the glowing screen and despatches a black dot across an expanse of grey sky to pass between two tall white posts. The commentators are besides themselves with escalating declarations of amazement and admiration. The mark, the kick, the goal and the player who made them are deemed to be worthy of inscription in the record books. The boy imagines a Saint Peter like figure gravely inscribing with a quill pen made from an enormous ostrich feather. "Good one," he says, moving to warm his backside by the fire.

"Lucky," says Dad.

Yes, lucky. Again.

Dad joins Janice and the younger boys at the window, drawing back the curtains to find the kids finishing off the pieces of toast Janice broke off for them. "Can we go out?" Dennis pleads. "Can we?"

Dad lets out a soft laugh. "Mum'll have me guts for garters if I let you out in that lot: In your pyjamas! Your toes'll freeze and drop off. Besides, it'll be there in the morning, don't worry about that. You can have all the snow you like then."

"Wacko!" sings the littlest. "Will it, Dad? True? Be there in the morning? We can make a snowman!"

The father rumples his child's not quite dry hair. "Boy, you can make all the snowmen you like, but right now you get back in front of that fire and dry this mop before you catch your death-o-cold. And you," he turns to his eldest, "can get another arm-load of wood in before washing up for tea."

"It's on the table!" Mum yells from the next room but the kids scamper to follow Roger to the back steps.

"Do you think there'll be much on the ground in the morning?" Janice asks, still gazing out the window.

"Dunno Love," her father replies as he pokes the fire back to life. And then, straightening up to look at the girl's back, "Probably. Could easily be quite a bit. I reckon we could just about organise a snowman. Whad'ya say?"

The girl shrugs and remains fixed by the window. "Well," her father announces with a clap of hands, "better eat." Watching the last moments of the Collingwood-Carlton highlights replay, he sidles to the door. A cigarette advertisement begins and he is gone. *Twenty-one great tobaccos make twenty wonderful smokes.* After a moment the girl huffs on the cold glass and there draws a heart.

Roger knees open the door and crashes a load of wood into the box beside the hearth. He stands by the fire gathering his breath. "Do us a favour?" he pants with what he considers jocular blandishment.

Janice places her hand over the misted heart and half turns her head. Her brother steps toward her and lowers his voice. "Ask Mum," he sez, "for us to watch *Twilight Zone* tonight. Bloody ol' Jo always gets *Gunsmoke*. It's my turn for a change. But you ask 'cos ... "

"It's on the table." Mum's high pitched yell carries an insistence dangerous to ignore. Roger responds automatically, instantly off like the robber's dog, but his sister lingers to carefully wipe away any trace of her breath's condensation.

"Jan-*ice!*"

The kids are sitting either side of Auntie Jo, pretending hiccups. When the old lady is finally distracted from shredding toast into her soup, she expertly administers stinging, finger-tip flicks to their ears. The youngest sniffles but quickly settles when Mum says he deserved it and she'll give him something to really bawl about if he doesn't pipe down and clean up his bowl.

Dad slurps and pulls a funny face. Collingwood won. Lucky.

Nunga's noxious grey bomb grumbles to the kerb a few doors down from the superette bottle shop. He kills the motor, lights a fag and eases himself down until the curly crown of his scurfy dolichocephalic head rests on the back of the seat and his bony knees nudge the steering wheel. Smoke streams from his nostrils as he studies the rain purling down the windscreen. He hears Roger, sprawled in the back seat, light up and toss his packet across to Mike, lolling against the front passenger door.

"So ..." Nunga drawls through a knowing grin. "Roger the Dodger. Here we all are again. Saturdee arvo cruisin' in Nung-ah's good ol' Velox. Few smokes, couple o bottles, bit of a natter, maybe some pervin' — not doing no harm to a livin', breathin' soul. Good as gold. Jist three little lambs. And Rodgie's layin' low in the back seat in case someone might see 'im. Dearie, dearie me. Wot a bloomin' disgrace that'd be."

Mike sniggers. Roger winces and flushes. "Not my fault."

"Honest, Rodgie-Dodge, I oughta go round your place and have a bit of a word with that old lady of yours. Sort her right out. Ask her how come she thinks I'm the one leading her precious lad astray. What about you'n'yer cousin Whoosha? Shit-a-brick, if she only knew the half o' what you two got up to of your own accord — poor old girl'd have a heart attack!" He thumps Mike's knee and crows with roisterous abandon.

Then snaps off the merriment. "Yeah... we could tell her a thing or two. Open her eyes. Couldn't we? Aye Mike?"

"For sure. Could too. You said it Nunga."

Nunga blows a wobbly smoke ring. The hours of mirrored practice are finally paying off.

"Youse are lucky," Roger whinges, "your olds don't care what you do. At least this way I can get out sometimes. But if she ... oh boy. She'd put me on the chain for keeps."

"Yeah, well," Nunga agrees with something like sympathy. "A hard one, your old chook. Mind you, getting stuck with that loony auntie of hers couldn't have done much for her temper! Jesus! What a family!"

More hooting, whooping, clapping and slapping of thighs. "Yeah, an' speaking of ... How old's that sister of yours? Young Janice. Saw her ridin' her bike home from school the other day. Gettin' ripe, Rodge, nice and juicy ripe, is Jan-nice. Tried slippin' her one, have we, mmmm?"

"Don't be ... "

"What? Don't be what?"

"Stupid?"

"Oooh ah. Stupid is it? Watch your language back there, Sport."

Mike titters. And then with sing-song mockery: "There was a young lady from Cape Cod, who thought all her children came from God. But it was not the Almighty, who lifted her nightie — it was ROGER THE LODGER, THE SOD!"

Sniggering and shoving in the front.

"Janice's only fourteen. Leave off about her."

"Touchy. Touch-ee. Four-teen! Lead me to it!"

The silence curdles.

Nunga turns his leering face to slowly wink at Mike. "Fourteen goin' on fifteen. Only asked ... I mean, if she's still a bit shy, well ... gently Bently, we aren't pushy. But you can tell us, cos we're your mates." A high giggle from Mike. "Now don't go gettin' too excited and playin' wiff yerself there Mike. Settle down, yer dirty little mongrel. Come on Rodge, tell us. Don't be bashful. Lots of blokes start by rootin' their little sisters. My sister was too old, so I missed out ... well, I used to perv on the bitch and all that caper. But *you!* You've got honey in the pot. An' going to waste! Tell yer! Col Rawlings — classic case — was rootin' his sister for years. Fuckin' wonder he didn't get her up the duff. Started on her when she was thirteen. Mind you ... old Col'd put his dick about just about anywhere. He was shaggin' the calves out on his uncle's farm."

"Cor!"

"True! I know that for a fact. For a fact. I got it from his cousins. They reckon they couldn't keep him away. Mind you, I reckon they taught him how to do it. Dirty bastards."

"Rawlings used to let the White Knight suck 'im off," offers Mike.

"So I heard. Still at it, probably. Ah, yes, matter of fact, saw the White Knight cruise on by in the Valiant the other day. Gave me a wave! I hear he gives the young 'uns a few bob to keep 'em quiet. You better watch out Rodge, the White Knight might get to hear you're not interested in sheilas and in need of a bit of cash. The White Knight always gets his man in the end!"

"He'll get you, he'll get you in the e-end-d — oh yeah."

"You two'd know."

"Ooooh ah!"

"Janice'd tell for sure."

"Pity 'bout that. We'll keep her under review. Under surveillance. But ... anyway. So! Who's got the dough ray me around here? Let's grab some booze and get moving."

Mike's pimply face slides into an apologetic grin as his hand emerges from the deep pocket of his dirty brown duffle coat with a roiling clutch of small change. He plucks a ruffled magazine from the glovebox, gingerly spreads it on the seat between himself and the glowering

Nunga and dumps the heavy money down for sorting and counting. His hand returns to the still bulging pocket and produces another assortment of low value coins.

Nunga snorts disgust and closes his narrow eyes. "Milk money!" He sits up straight and rants at Mike. "Told yer before — not takin' that kinda shrapnel in to buy grog. Look a proper dill. Told you before — *you* get it changed! Rodge, just *look* at this crap! Fuck's sake! Need a bloody wheelbarrow!"

"Only got it last night! Fair goes, can't change it near my place. People talking as it is."

"You fuckin' well could've gone into town and got Roger to change it in the fruit shop."

"Had to stay home an' chop wood an' stuff this morning."

"Rodge! Look at this, will yer? Com'n, you change some of this shit. You got a couple of two-bob bits there ... for Christ's sake, help us out here."

Roger looks over the seat at the slew of coins. "You've been ... busy."

"Yeah..." Nunga grudgingly admits. "A few streets worth there right enough."

"Give me four bob's worth. I'll change it at the shop."

"You're on a good thing in the good old Fruit Palace. Makin' a fair screw on the side?"

"Not as easy as it looks. Charlie's got his eyes peeled lately. I gotta be careful. He counts the cartons in the safe — keeps all the smokes in a bloody great monster old safe under the stairs. I gotta nick 'em from the display racks in the shop, all up there at the front under that whoppin' great fluoro light. *And* he's loading the racks himself."

"Yeah!"

"Not so easy any more. I mean, he don't mind me knocking off the odd packet for meself, but he draws the line at cartons. I've knocked off selling at school. Johnny Nelson put on a bit of an act."

"Yeah?! What a prick! Gettin' cheap fags for ages ... bit of gratitude wouldn't hurt him. Now ... Oh, for fuck's sake! Jist gimme the silver! What've we got in silver?"

"Six an' nine."

"Six and bloody nine pence ... need another nine pence for three beers. Ah shit, gimme it outta that crap! Milk money! Fair dinkum, there's gotta be something easier. Gotta be!" He loads the coins into his own coat pocket. "Go and get the White Knight's money! Quicker 'n' safer 'n' more fun than stealing milk money." His long, knuckly fingers curl around the door handle, his swarthy chin dips forward and his knees swing sideways so — cluntsk — the door opens and he rolls gangster style from his seat to crouch on the rain sprayed road, one hand holding the open door. With clenched teeth — *he he he* — he pulls the pin from the grenade, tosses it into Mike's lap and slams the door. He dashes to the front of the vehicle, takes up the well known pose of a man operating a Tommy Gun and rapidly riddles all and sundry — *dut ah dut ah dut dut dut*. From behind the steel-backed seat Roger returns fire with a long barrel Luger. Mike gets his window down and with a last shuddering stretch of desperation pitches the (he sez) unexploded grenade back at Nunga. Both sides claim victory as Nunga mounts the cement footpath and lopes toward the bottle shop. He's back a few minutes later with a large brown paper bag in the crook of his arm. As they drive away he pulls a small bottle of vodka from his coat's secret inside pocket. "The old bastard must be blind," he brays above the slish-slush of wagging wipers and the motor's accelerating howl. "Coulda sworn he saw me that time!"

"But he didn't!"

"Hah!" Nunga finds third and tramps it. "Not this rooster," he exults, "not in a million fuckin' years."

The classroom lights have been on all the dull day long. Squabbling tatters of grey and black, demented witches, ride the bone-aching southerly over the school's dark orange tile roof. Quick, vicious rain squalls pounce against the second-floor windows as, gaze fixed on the Turner print at the back of the room, Mr Morris intones *Dover Beach* at the eleven sulky girls and thirteen sullen boys of 5C. It is, he knows after almost twenty years of teaching, a profoundly pointless performance; and yet, harmless drudge, he continues to toil in Hope's delusive mine.

Halfway through the last verse — on 'Hath really neither joy' et cetera — the teacher's tired brown eyes glimpse Ryan and Walker, jaws set, surreptitiously struggling over something under their back row desk. Mr Morris would rather not be bothered with the business of exposing whatever it is the scrug pair are tugging back and forth: In all probability a tattered copy of *Man Magazine* with every second tart's airbrushed pubic hair crudely shaded back with lead pencil — utterly predictable and vile. No, he does not miss a sonorous beat, but by 'Where ignorant armies clash by night' he is quizzically staring at the offending duo, who, in turn, earnestly study Matthew Arnold's deathless words.

"Well now," Mr Morris allows himself a conspiratorial nod to Turner, "Master Walker. Could I have your attention?"

"Sir?"

The teacher stares at the student. Waiting.

"Sir," Roger offers, "Michael says he saw a flying saucer, Sir. Night before last, Sir."

A flock of sniggers swirl about the room.

Mr Morris doesn't blink. The class stills. "I wonder,

Master Walker, could your perfervid imagination and penetrating perspicacity be applied to enlighten the rest of the class as to what the poet is saying in the last stanza?"

Feet move. Titters and shuffles eddy. 5C understand that big words are sarcasm, and in sarcasm there is a whiff of blood.

Roger shifts his boots about and concentrates his shoulders. His eyes skip the lines like a stone over water. "Sir ..." he looks up, beaming insight, "I think he's saying things are pretty crook all over!"

"Things *are* pretty crook indeed." Mr Morris affects drollery to ripple further titters through the girls. "And what does Arnold suggest we do about this parlous state of affairs?"

Roger frowns into the text, seeking an elusive clue. "Sir," he brightens at last, "that'll be the first bit — like, what he sez to his girlfriend about stickin' together." Roger's grin is positively lickerous.

The entire class have their noses a few inches above School Inspector Arnold's words, studiously pondering the question of how, exactly, we must 'be true to one another'. Baff boom, the fidgety wind bumps and buffets the high window frames. Turning to ponder the stormy sky, the fretful tossing of bare trees, Mr Morris puts his hands behind his narrow back and rocks on his feet. The moon, he muses was a ghostly galleon. Alfred Noyes, he likes to tell people, is a distant relation on the distaff. *Was* a distant relation. He thinks, in what he considers to be an intellectual way, about how Fate's cruel arrows are deflected until their eventual mark is quite random, perhaps even innocent — the rain falls on the just and the unjust.

The rain falls. Five minutes to the end of the class, to the end of the day. Time enough to teach someone a lesson, to have a little sport, a divertissement: "Walker ... stand, please."

Another wave of nervy hilarity surges when Roger knocks his knee as he stands out from his desk. Watching Mr Morris's motionless back, Mike snatches the magazine, warm from Roger's bum, and slips it under his own posterior. Matters wait a moment before Mr Morris turns to face his prey. "Come on!" he suddenly jumps to bluff impatience. "We haven't all day. Explain what you meant about 'stickin' together'. And, please, a coherent answer!"

"Don't know. Sir."

"Don't know!?" Incredulous scoff. "Master Walker's stuck for an answer!" The predictable answering lick of laughter rises and falls. "Well then, consider the rule, the very simple rule: 'each other' applies to two persons, animals, or things; 'one another' to three or more. What do we make of that in reference to this poem?"

"Well ... sorta, like ... everybody has to look after everyone else, I suppose, Sir."

"You suppose. Dear me! Do we detect a trace of a blush 'pon yon fair youth's downy cheek? Don't tell us Walker is embarrassed by something in a mouldy old poem?"

The girls, lips parted, cast longer looks at the victim. He really is blushing now.

Baff, says the gusting wind. Boom, says the annoyed window.

"Bring your book to the front of the class," says Mr Morris, soft with threat. "Come along — nice, clear voice, be confident — read the last verse."

"Ah! Love! Let us be true. To one another."

Herr Professor's arm shoots up in Nazi salute to call *Halt*. "Look at the *punct-u*-ation!"

Roger catches Mary Clarke's bright eye and turns beetroot. Mary Clarke is one of those honey-skin girls who, wearing the shortest skirt permissible, keep their hands warm by stretching the sleeves of their school pullovers down over their fists; an action that incidentally stretches the fabric tight over their budding breasts.

"Listen ...

Ah, love, let us be true
To one another! for the world, which seems
To lie before us ...

Let your breath follow the poem's rhythm. Watch the punctuation. Now go on, go on."

Roger swallows and takes a deep breath.

"Ah love ... let us be true ... to one an-*other*!"

"*Ah, love, let us be true* — let it flow, Walker, let-it-flow."

And so on until the sorry joke is stopped by the bell.

"Saved by the bell, Walker! Practice it over the weekend. Rehearse before a mirror, in the bath." Mr Morris's smile does not reveal his teeth. "We'll hear you on Monday. Something to which the rest of us may look forward. Ryan, I want you to wait back." He claps his hands, "Class dismissed."

Just think, next term they've got *Lord of the Flies*.

Viewed from the top of the eroded clay embankment, from the vantage of the Jap pillbox, the round clumps of golden furze stud the lawn smooth, emerald gully floor as the buffers of a pinball table. Sheltered from the steady breeze, the tableau's deep drowse is marked only by the slow alternation of light and shadow as a procession of cloud pillows drift across the infinitely blue heaven.

"Cover me," Nunga growls like Lee Marvin (who he thinks he resembles), and crouches to dash for the next stand of furze. Both hands firmly holding the twenty-two, he charges out as Roger and Mike lop quartz grenades and pump their Winchesters at the fortress under siege. He flings himself down into a rollover that lands him in the prone marksman position. A grey shadow with a flash of white breaks cover. Nunga is instantly to the kneeling position.

Aim — fire!

The rabbit tosses sideways into an off-balance somersault. The gully claps shut over the flat report. Silence holds its breath.

Nunga stands to draw back the bolt. An empty cartridge springs bright into the afternoon light. Fishing in his shirt pocket for another bullet, he starts towards his kill.

The others run up behind him, "Got 'im!"

"Through the head," Nunga purrs, and with a casualness meant to be dramatic he eases the bolt home.

"Jeez! What a shot!"

"Watch out the wind don't change on yer there Mike," sez Nunga, the embodiment of raffish wit. "Yer eyes are stickin' out like pickled onions — could knock 'em off with sticks."

"But ... " Mike shakes his head and laughs. He picks up the dead rabbit, runs his hand down its warm underside and pronounces the pelt a good one.

"Oughta bring your ferrets out here."

"Nah ... " Mike vaguely nods at the rank gorse. "Lose 'em in this sorta stuff." With his free hand he deftly opens his pocket knife, slits a hind leg behind the tendon and splices through the other paw. He hefts the carcass to judge the weight and once more caress the downy white belly.

Nunga lays down his rifle and lights a smoke. He's pleased, very pleased with himself. He snaps his fingers and holds out his hand to Roger, who has been assigned the job of minding the bottle of Marsala.

The rabbit is gently laid on the grass beside the rifle. The plonk swigging, fag puffing trio stand around and admire their prize. Nunga rewards himself with an extra chug before corking the brown bottle and passing it back to Roger. The quiet fellowship of hunters prevails.

Mike is offered a couple of shots if he'll gut the catch. In less than a minute he is displaying the clean, pink bunny liver and declaring the same to be free of myxo. As he wipes his knife and hands on the grass he scans the edge of the nearest thicket, soon discovering the run for which the rabbit was headed. He moves closer and examines the patch of earth ... free of tracks and somehow littered with too many twigs. He carefully lifts a limb of the thorny bush and sees the stake and its attached chain — a trap.

Nunga springs the serrated jaws with a lump of quartz and sez he's saved Bugs from a fate-worse-than-death. "These things," he sanctimoniously declares, "are worse than ferrets."

Mike, his chance at the rifle on the line, is not provoked. He wonders aloud who might have set the trap, judging it to have been set that very day.

"Someone probably sets a whole string of them in here," sez Nunga. "Some old geezer who ... " He grabs his gun and sweeps the embankments, coming to rest on a particularly large and dense clump of furze halfway up the gully throat. "Someone," he murmurs, "who's probably watching us right now."

"Arrh yeah ... sure Nunga. And who's that then?" jeers Mike.

Never lowering his aim from the thicket at the top of the gully, Nunga's face slowly lights with radiant wickedness. "Apple Jack, of course."

The boys freeze and follow his aim. They have just managed to force out nervous laughter when he fires. He lowers his gun to grin at their shocked faces. Mike has jumped about a foot and a half backwards, but nobody notices.

"*Jeez-us*! What if there were someone up there? Shit-a-brick!"

"It sure *looks* like you two just shit a couple o' bricks!" Nunga cackles and pulls a strained face. All at once the three of them are reeling with uncontrollable, mindless laughter.

As when he plays scary games with the kids, he holds himself very still in the dark passage, breathing shallow through his open mouth. He listens. Auntie Jo's snores ascend to suspend her over a silent zenith, then plummet into snotty snorts and thin whistles. Her sleep is as deep as that of the kids: Jo always cleans up the sherry when Mum and Dad leave her to mind the fort. He can hardly stop himself spluttering a mad giggle. His finger tips confirm Jo's closed door and he moves his weight to creep down and across the passage — one, two, three soundless stork strides — to feel the door jamb of Janice's room. He listens. Cheek and shoulder braced against the door, he grips the knob with both hands to lift it as he turns ... through the inch gap of secret darkness he smells Coty powder, warm linen, rising bread and the ozone of a really, really serious game. His breath trembles. He allows the door knob and catch to ease back. He presses his sweaty palms to the front of his pyjamas and listens. His ears roar in beat to his heart thump and the heat of his erect dick. He licks his lips and pushes open the door. "You awake?" he whispers, hoarsely, and steps across the threshold of all that his mother never taught him.

"Nicky-whoop Roger." As hard and bright as frost. "Get out of my room!"

He closes the door behind him.

"But, but, I just wanna talk, I just ... "

"But nothing. Keep away from me or I'll tell Mum."

"Aawh, Jeez! Don't go off your face. Blab to Mum and I'll tell her about ... "

"Say what you like. Get *out* of my room!"

He goes, quietly, his dick radiating heat in the dark.

Today's the day.

The sun has licked off the skim of frost and everything under heaven knows it's going to be a fine day. Flowers are smiling, bugs are hopping and racing about, the birds are stuffing their faces and chirping and warbling to their precious little hearts' content — all's a-sparkle in the sweet air!

Roger the Dodger, pedalling like a mad thing and generating fanciful sound effects, screams off Wellington Parade slope to sweep by the Titanic memorial bandstand and recklessly cut into the broad concourse of Sturt Street. The grand old Town Hall clock merrily-merrily dongs out seven o'clock and our jockeying cyclist, fresh-faced to the lettuce crisp morning, is, yet again, as usual, late for work.

Not that he's too worried. As on every other Saturday morning, Charlie rants and raves for the thirty seconds it takes Roger to dismount, shove his bike's front wheel in the rack on the pavement out front and dash down the long, narrow shop to hang his duffle coat behind the backroom door. Then, turning on the moment, one big hand gripping Roger's shoulder and the other gesticulating in true costermonger style, Charlie launches — "Now listen!" — into detailed instructions as to the construction of the cauliflower leaf borders, crunchy apple terraces, firm banana cascades, juicy orange pyramids and snowy cauliflower slopes of the Alfred Fruit Palace & Milk Bar's showy street display.

While the artful youth builds the man's cornucopian

vision, that worthy withdraws to his office alcove behind the pinball machines, where he creates the day's price cards. Charlie is especially proud of his poster paint lettering skills and especially fond of the word *Especial!*, it flashes like a trademark across the top of more than half of his signs. He also deploys *Choice!* and *Select!*; especially when he has something not quite in season — like that single box of over-priced (*Select!!*) white heart cherries, arrived by last night's express.

Roger has the front display done to Charlie's satisfaction and has almost finished filling the under-counter bins with dusty spuds, brown onions and heavy, uncut pumpkins by the time the rest of the Saturday morning crew trot in shortly before eight. Old Helen, tall and sprightly, dark blue genteel cardigan over light blue serviceable smock, greets Roger with an indulgent nod and a brisk smile. Tiny Gwen, late thirties, cheeks like apples and breasts like cantaloupes, as plump and fizzy as a sparrow, gleefully pinches his bum as she brushes by. Young Denise, smock hem much, much higher than Helen would prefer for a nice young Catholic girl, gives him a flirty wink and a warm, easy laugh such as would break a grown man's heart. Everybody, even the stray early customers he breaks off to serve, remarks on the unbounded loveliness of the day. *Fresh!* Everything is so fresh! Charlie wishes he had taken the risk and ordered that second box of cherries. They would have sold themselves on a perfect day like today.

But Charlie does have a problem. There is a dreadful cavity in his otherwise beaming front display. Like all good fruit and vegie men, he knows a shop without *Especial!* tomatoes and *Fresh!* lettuces is the show without Punch. He runs his comb through his Brylcreemed hair, rewashes his hands and adjusts his clean white apron to welcome his customers. But by a quarter to nine he is out in the back lane, pacing and cursing because Bluey and Simmo are running late in returning from Melbourne with the day's supply of, among other things, tomatoes and lettuce. If they don't turn up soon sales will be lost; worse still, there could be quantities of those perishables left over to be thrown out cheap on Monday. Charlie mutters as he visualises blue *Cooking!* and *Cheap!!* signs on the over-ripe tomatoes. He lights another cigarette and kicks the cat by calling Roger out to sort soft drink bottles in the back lane with orders to stop that and bring a crate of lettuce through to the shop immediately the truck arrives. Roger hopes that'll be any minute because if Bluey and Simmo don't show before nine o'clock Charlie's stroppy mood will be set for the day.

As it happens the big Bedford lurches up the lane bang on the hour. Charlie is out venting spleen before Roger can undo the first knot of the tarp, before Bluey and Simmo are even down from the cab to stretch their legs. They obviously expected Charlie's scene because Simmo promptly commences his own line of invective against the wholesaler who held them up, while Bluey prattles about city traffic — so that three of the quartet undoing the tarp are running their own discursive monologues of woe. Roger, working the same side of the truck as Simmo, can't help smirking when the truckie's offsider lapses into nodding his head and rolling his eyes in a perfect take-off of Charlie. The two barely have time to put on a straight face before the man himself is around their side wanting to know what's the bloody hold-up.

With Charlie out of the way — up front on the lookout for any old duck who'd dare squeeze his *Especial Firm!* tomatoes — unloading can proceed in correct order and at a sensible pace. Simmo on the truck tray, Roger in the middle, Bluey stacking; they get into the rhythm of turn, catch and swing to move eight dozen brute heavy cabbages. Then it's four dozen cauliflowers. They work up a healthy sweat in the morning sun. A breather to figure out where to put things and then back into it shouldering smooth deal cases of Valencia oranges from Riverland, apples from Tasmania, carrots from Gippsland, pears from Shepparton; and in rough, splintery crates — bananas from faraway Queensland. Fresh fruit and vegetables for today, for tomorrow, for next week.

After smoko he's back in the shop replenishing stacks and bins. By mid-morning customers are waiting to be served. Charlie and his Girls are flat out to the jolly ding-a-ling of the till and the snap, riffle, plop of brown paper bags. Before long Roger is cutting up Ironbark pumpkin for one of Helen's customers, and from there it's only a quick jut of Charlie's jaw to "Next Please".

Roger likes serving. It's so easy to be good at it. Also, he can control the tone and pace of the transaction and, being at the customer's disposal, not even Charlie will interfere. Hustle-bustle, pencilled arithmetic, silver exchanged for coppers, three bags full Sir.

Mike comes into the shop just after eleven o'clock rings over the cheerful, clean town. He edges through the crush at the front and, catching his mate's eye, sidles towards the Milk Bar section at the rear, where he asks for change for the pinball. Coppers are turned into silver and the transaction leaves that till a shilling short. Sometime in the next busy hour Roger must put the diddle right by under-ringing sales without Charlie noticing. Mike tells him Nunga will pick them up from the usual place at the usual time. Today's the day they're going to try out the ferrets at a few selected locations near Chinaman's Hill.

Most shops close at midday and by quarter to one Sturt Street is drifting into the sleeping dog quiet of a country town afternoon. The farmers who propped against one another's utes to rub tobacco in the hollow of their hands and yarn while their floral pattern wives handled Charlie's tomatoes — they're either driving home or picnicking on town pies by the lake; the housewives who lugged cane shopping baskets and whingeing kids from butcher to grocer to baker to green-grocer to chemist to that nice little New Australian shoe-repair man — they're now rushing to get their husbands' lunches on the table, to get them out of their hair and off to the footy semi-final (and with the younger kids off to the matinee at the Regal there'll be time to read the paper and maybe even have a nap); Helen, Gwen and Denise have knocked off and Charlie is counting his takings, leaving Roger, the Dodger, to mop the floor before old Clive comes in to take watch for the afternoon.

A trio of North Tech scallywags looking for a go on the pinball troop across the wet linoleum. Our boy, mostly somewhere else anyway, refuses to be stirred and just gets on with wiping over their tracks. After all, he's hidden two packets of smokes in his coat and in fifteen minutes Charlie is going to pay him twenty-two and six — money in his pocket and free for the rest of the day.

They leave their bikes in the Ryans' shed and hurry to meet Nunga, who doesn't like waiting. Mike's ferret box bump bumps against his hip as they stride up the street. Roger wolfs a meat pie, performing the antic manoeuvre of holding the pie at ear level and twisting his head to slurp a glistening dollop of tepid gravy from the soggy underside, all done without the slightest hesitation in or disturbance to his swaggering gait.

"Hun-*gry*!"

"Could eat a horse."

"Probably are. Or worse. Hear about the joker found a frog in a Chico roll? Rank! Even the dogs wouldn't eat it."

"Get knotted!"

Left, right, march along.

Fractious as ever, the '54 Vauxhall Velox brumbles up to cruise level on the opposite side of the road. One hand on the wheel, the other draped out the window, Nunga, cigarette clenched between bared teeth, studies his accomplices from behind shiny black sunglasses. *New* shades. No amount of Cool can disguise how greatly pleased he is with himself and his bulbous dark, dark-glasses. A narrow spun-metal comb — aluminium oxide purple — preens his sleek head. Nobody is going to tell him, but he has achieved a quite remarkable resemblance to a praying mantis.

"Rrrrocka!" Roger hails him with the deepest and growliest voice he can manage. Mike chimes in and together they chant, "Rockar! Rockar! Rockar!"

Ten minutes later, down a dirt track at the back of Chinaman's Hill, unseen crows cark and cor as Nunga parks his grey bomb out of sight behind a century-old mullock heap encircled by big, rough-barked Douglas firs, dark and redolent in the day's warm stillness.

Tiger butterflies, wanderers, flicker above the lower boughs.

Sunglasses in place, the twenty-two rifle slung over his shoulder, Nunga leads his troops up the switch-back path to the top of the mullock; from where, between the heads of the trees, they survey their domain, their hunting ground.

It's all Crown Reserve around here. The poppet heads that spewed the bare conical hills of grey clay mullock were dismantled generations ago, but the holes in the ground, now mostly hidden by clumps of furze, remain. To one side of the lookout the land runs more or less level, vestiges of The Rush muted by a century of weather and a coat of bright spring grass; only the half-dozen or so mullock heaps proclaim the real nature of the country. Around the other way, towards Chinaman's Hill, or what's left of it, the damage is more spectacular. Scene of the most intensive digging, the hill was torn apart, its original shape now and forever more a mystery. What remains is a dangerous maze of cuts, concealed pits, unmarked vertical and horizontal shafts, erosion gullies and secret places.

On top of the world, they light cigarettes, swig Marsala and scan the vista for signs of life. Not a soul in sight. Mike points to a few places where he'd be prepared to try his ferrets, but Nunga interrupts him to identify enemy positions along the jig-saw crest of Chinaman's Hill. They've played war games since they started primary school, but Nunga (kicked out of School Cadets for loading 303s with blanks and quartz gravel) has lately burgeoned into quite the military tactician. He's actually read a book on the subject. Truth is: he's seriously thinking of joining up next year and getting himself a plane ride to Saigon for some real action — and blow jobs galore! He tells his platoon he may have to call in an airstrike and drop some *nay*-palm on Charlie. Mike and Roger are making supporting dialogue when Nunga announces he's already made up four *nay*-palm bombs — they're in the boot of the Velox.

Nobody says anything. They know Nunga was shown how to make petrol bombs last summer by Whoosh, Roger's cousin Larry, the one mixed up in that nasty business over at Kyneton.

Yes, Whoosh and his fires ... but that's another story.

So, anyway ... not long after, armed with the loaded twenty-two, the flagon of Marsala, Mike's squirming ferrets, the petrol bombs, grenades, bazookas and all the small arms imaginable, they stand atop the broken back ridge, scanning the jumble of furze infested gullies spilling away to meet the forest of spreading oaks marching out from the back of the park. Beyond the splendid bright green of new leaves are the shaded lawns of the park proper. To one side, bounded by a bluestone shore, the brimming lake adamantly remains slate grey beneath a deep blue sky. Beyond all, serene and silent with distance, is the panorama — the streets and homes — of the contented town.

A faraway breeze caresses Roger's silky hair. Skylarks wheel and chitter unnoticed. Everything under heaven rejoices in the sweetness of its raw existence.

Mike's sharp eyes spy the tremble slowly passing through the furze. He gives a low whistle and crouches to point down a narrow, crooked gully dropping steeply from one side of the next knob of the ridge. Beneath the bushes skirting the base of the yellow cliff, something is making its way along a hidden path. Where the cliff tucks away they have a sudden glimpse of the crown of a hat, an old hat.

"Well, wha'd'ya know ..." and Nunga flashes his mates a wily grin. He snatches his walkie-talkie into existence and reports to HQ. "Subject under surveillance. Proceeding to locate hideout and gold stash. Over."

"Ssshsquarrrhshharrr — bip bip bip — arrhgha hahgarrrr."

"Eye eye, Sore. Read you. Will do. Repeat: Will do. Ova'n'knout." He clicks off the transceiver and sizes up his men. "Well, you heard — time to meet the Boogieman. Let's go. Single file. Y'ho!"

They dodge from cover to cover down and along the front of the ridge until, opposite the gully where they shot the rabbit and found one of Apple Jack's traps, Nunga spots the innocent gap between bushes. A prickly frond is drawn aside to expose the sinewy brown limbs, the dusty, sickly-sweet interior of furze thickets — and there, you'll have to crawl to avoid multiple scratches, is the entrance to the trail. Born and bred in the briar patch, Nunga taps his shades into place and curls his top lip, displaying his left side canine.

Open Sesame.

In they go — one, two, three little devils. The frond swishes behind and they are in another world. The ferrets scratch and turn in their box.

"You can leave them bastards here," Nunga nods at the box. "Better bring one of those though," and his rifle swings over the outline of the petrol and oil filled milk bottles standing in the sugarbag at Roger's side.

Mike, excited, nervous, asks, "Why? What're we gunna do?"

The platoon commander stiffens fingers to a scout salute. "Be prepared."

"Yeah, but ... like, it's so dry in here and I don't wanna, you know, hurt no one and get into trouble or anything like that."

Nunga regards Mike for a long moment before answering. "Trouble? We're only gonna *talk* to the old bastard! Or-right? Bring the grog an' we'll give 'im a drink if it makes yer happy. Not turnin' chicken on us, are yer?"

"Course not!" Flustering indignation.

"Or-right, that's good. Listen, we might have to give 'im a bloody good fright — but we won't hurt 'im. Put the breeze up the old bastard, that's all." Again, the fox grin. "But, yer know, only if he gets stroppy. Now, come on. Keep the racket down and watch out for bloody traps. Never know, old cunt might have something bigger than a rabbit trap in here."

They ease through to the base of the yellow cliff. Edging forward with their backs to the wall and their heads tilted sideways under the thorny canopy they file along the path; Nunga leads and Roger brings up the rear. Every so often the thicket has been slashed to allow passage. But not much, it's a tight fit. Sweat stings scratches and streaks dust down their necks. They rest, breathing hard, at the bend where they saw the hat. Here they can see the sky. Here they can see the opposite side of the gully, and realise that there's no other way into this place. No other way out.

The gully wall turn is so sharp and perpendicular it looks like the work of a mason, like the corner of a building. You have to edge right up to it and peep around like they do in gangster films. That's the way Nunga does it. It's called 'stealing a look'.

"D'ya see 'im?" Mike jostles to peer around his leader.

Nunga's lips compress to a hard line of disgust. He has only to prod Mike's shoulder with the tip of a rigid index finger for the kid to realise his mistake.

Nunga readjusts his sunnies and, in one step, rounds the bend. The others jostle close behind him.

The view is not quite what they expected. The gully has not eroded out of Chinaman's Hill ridge in the usual manner, rather, it cuts back in deep to form a furze filled hollow surrounded by fifty-foot walls — a man-made box canyon.

"Must've been a lot of gold in here," Nunga murmurs to himself.

A third of the way up in one corner is the entrance to an old tunnel, a steep spew of tailings falling from its dark mouth. Nunga's eyes trace along the path to the adit and he sees there is no way anyone could creep up on someone sitting back inside the mine. Mike and Roger crowd his back, nudging him forward. The notion of a trap twists below his thoughts. He clutches his rifle to his chest.

"Betcha that tunnel goes right through the ridge."

"Betcha he's watchin' us."

"Shut the fuck up. Here, gimme that grog. Follow me and keep your eyes peeled."

"Suppose he's got a gun."

Nunga stops dead in his tracks. Mike and Roger bump into his back. He lowers his glasses until they perch on the tip of his long nose. He considers the steady darkness of the mine aiming straight at him.

"He won't have a gun," sez Roger.

"Why not? Nunga has."

"Yeah, but, even if he has, why should he use it?"

"Yeah, but ... "

"Yeah, but nuthin'! Don't be a blithering berk all yer life," sez Nunga. "Any more bright ideas, *brain*-box — you can keep 'em to yerself. Now quit crowding me. Here, carry this while I go on ahead with the booze."

"*I'm* not holding the gun!"

"Well get outta the way then. Here, Rodge, just sling it over your shoulder. No sense in, you know, upsetting anyone."

"Maybe, you know ..." Mike's voice is too high and too loud. "I mean, what'da we wanna talk to him for anyway? I mean, maybe we oughta just, ya know ... go back."

"G'on then — piss off!" Nunga musters all of his contempt. "We're not stoppin' yer. Christ Almighty! I'm just gunna talk to the old boy, that's all. He might have something to say worth hearing! I'll ask him the best place to go rabbitin'. Or-right! What's yer problem with that?"

"I dunno, but ... "

"Keep yer bloody voice down! All this yabbering — bloke can't hardly hear himself think. You dun-no! You're right about that much. You dunno nuffin'. Shut yer trap or piss off."

But Mike doesn't go back and Nunga doesn't go forward. They listen to the torpid dreams of the sun-trap hollow. In the pellucid stillness things are being pushed skew-whiff. Their mouths are dry, their backs are wet with sweat. It has hardened to a certainty that Apple Jack is watching them from his lair. That he has seen them bickering. That he has seen their fear.

Nunga licks his lips. "Yeah, well ... " He pokes his shades back up his schnoz, tells the others to stay put, and, flagon firmly in hand, sets off towards the dark hole in the cliff.

"Aye Mate!" He's halfway up the tailing spill, eyelevel with the tunnel floor, steadying himself with one hand gripping his forward, bent knee. "Aye Mate! Want a drink?" And he sloshes the purple plonk in the light green half–gallon bottle.

No answer.

"C'mon Mate." The plonk once more liberally sloshed. "Have a drink with us. Just a friendly swig."

Still. Silence.

"C'mon Mate. Shit! Rude to keep visitors way-*ting*." He turns to flash his funny fella grin at the boys.

Nobody sez Boo.

"Listen. We know yer in there. We'll be doin' some shootin' around here. Only tryin' to do the right thing by tellin' yer. That's fair enough, ain't it?"

"Clear off."

Nunga stares into the gloom, listening, trying to see with his ears. The voice has boomed with sonority and timbre gathered along the walls of the tunnel, but that hasn't masked the whisper of apprehension.

"How's that?" He cups his ear and moves up a couple of steps. "Didn't quite catch that. Come out where I can see yer."

"Stop! I'm warning you — get back!"

Nunga leers like a loon at his mates. "He's warning us. Jeez, fair shittin' meself!"

He's half turned back towards the tunnel when

something white flashes into the sunlight. In the first fraction of perception he thinks *bird*; then the fist sized lump of quartz clips his shades. It barely grazes his temple, but it smashes off his glasses and spills him down the scree of gravel tailings. At the bottom of his sprawling belly slide, legs in the furze, Nunga has lost his dark glasses, his dignity, his wind and a few square inches of skin. Face down, he lies for a moment in his cloud of pale dust. Against the odds, the flagon lies intact beside him. The shades are history. He feels his forehead, his eye, his cut cheek, his elbow ... his hands are bleeding and starting to sting. His curse is made with intense deliberation and rising inflection. He bawls: "You fuckin' dirty old *fucking CUNT!*"

The dog emerges to claim the high ground. A big, black curly-haired retriever, rangy with a bit of greyhound in him, lowers its head and snarls down at the prone Nunga. The mongrel obviously means business. Serious business.

Nobody knew Apple Jack had a dog.

Nunga gets up onto his knees. Grabs the flagon by the neck. "Call 'im off! We're going. Or-right? Don't want no trouble. Call 'im off! Or-right Mister?"

Roger unslings the rifle and half raises it.

A sharp whistle ricochets out of the mine. The black dog flicks his ears, licks his jowls, grumbles deep, turns an impatient circle and sits to watch his intended sport — who's slowly getting to his feet and watching right back.

Now the lanky lout l-l-lurches across the scribbling scree. He says not a word until he regains the path and takes his eyes off the dog long enough to see Mike and Roger retreating towards the corner. Such craven timidity draws forth the cry, "Wait! Wait for me!"

Muttering as he glances over his shoulder, Nunga makes his way towards his comrades-in-arms. When he's almost to them he again tells them to wait, only this time he speaks with quiet fury. Then the dog turns its head and wiggles its butt to acknowledge the man standing behind it. Nunga stops to stare at the tall figure wearing grey flannel trousers and a khaki shirt. Under his hat the man's face is a mask of shadow.

"Get going! Catch you around here again, I'll sool him onto you straight away." The voice has the texture of broken bricks.

Chalk-white with rage, Nunga reaches the boys. "I'll teach this fuckin' old bastard." He hands the flagon to Mike like it was a precious gift, plucks a cigarette and matches from Roger's shirt pocket and lights up. The boys gawk, silenced by the nasty cut below Nunga's left eye and the fury that ignores such a wound. "Gunna get that cunt, good'n'proper."

"Let's ..." Mike croaks. "C'mon, let's get outta here."

"We will, we will. Stop shittin' yerself!" With his back to the man, Nunga quietly takes the petrol bomb from Mike. "Listen. Do what I say and don't chicken out or I'll thump the livin' daylights outta you. Believe me, I will. Got it? Now, stop being a bloody sook."

Mike looks like he's about to blub, but he swallows and nods agreement. Roger seems dreamily calm, unconcerned.

Nunga smiles at them. Roger smiles back.

Nunga tells Mike to take the flagon and the rifle around the bend and wait for his call.

Mike is trembling as he takes the gun from Roger. "What're ya gunna do?"

"Get even," sez Nunga. "We're a gunna get even. Simple as that. Just act like you're leavin', but stay ready round the bend. Don't go runnin' away. Understand?"

Mike moves off. He looks back at the man and the dog. They haven't moved. Nunga has the fire bomb upturned, loosening the rag wick to well and truly soak it. Roger is picking up stones. Nunga squats as though to do the same, but in fact he's dusting his hands to remove spilt fuel.

The pair start to walk back up towards the mine. Although the narrow path is more open here, there is still enough cover to hide the bottle Nunga holds to his side.

The black dog stands and tenses. His master steps further into the light. "I told you to clear off. G'on! Get! I'll put the dog on ya!"

"Hang on a jiff there, Mate. Settle down, will ya?! What're you so snaky about anyway? Wha'd'yer have ta chuck that rock at me for?" Nunga keeps coming, Roger one step behind. "I wanna get me sunglasses back. OK?"

"Drop those stones! I'm warning you."

"What stones?" Nunga raises one arm to display a half-smoked cigarette.

The man comes up beside his bristling dog. The boys stop to take him in, to sum him up. Somewhere in his fifties, it's hard to judge his age, grey hair, slate-grey eyes, grey bristle — a gaunt, hard man with a face that has forgotten how to smile.

The dog is on his second bound down the tailings when the bottle with the fluttering, smoking rag shatters before him. He cannot avoid the dark honey splash — 75% petrol topped with oil. It's the oil that sticks. It fans up into the animal's face, soaks his chest, sprays along the exposed pink and grey skin of his belly. A soft *whump* — such a gentle sound — and it flashes alight everywhere at once. *Whoosh!* The dog gives one pathetic yelp before burning air scorches his throat, then his jaws are clamped as he thrashes and contorts to roll or twist from the tenacious flame. Finally, he gets to his feet and appears to shiver as a lazy, orange flame flows up his side and along his back. A frantic burst of speed races him up the slope towards his master and the mine. Half way up he folds and somersaults back into the furze, where he resumes his pitiful twists and turns.

One look at Apple Jack's face and the assailants scarper. Like startled rabbits they dash, freeze, then bolt another ten yards before freezing once more. They look back to see Apple Jack stride down the scree swinging a bloody great axe. They see it rise and fall twice. They hear it thunk into flesh and through bone. Nunga's lips quiver as he tries to explain something to himself.

Bloodied axe gripped across his chest, his face a leather mask, Apple Jack comes after them with long, steady strides.

They hurtle around the corner screaming at Mike, "He's got an axe! An axe!"

Oblivious to lacerations, they charge along the overgrown path to where they left the ferrets and the rest of the bombs. Nunga pulls the wicks and pours the mixture on the path, into the surrounding undergrowth. With the match poised to strike, he listens — the devil is coming along the hidden path. The flame jumps into the gorse, surging and crackling as the boys regain the open track along the ridge. Pungent white smoke streaked with dirty yellow suddenly surges into the air.

They run like billy-oh. Ferret box banging against his rump, Mike keeps asking what happened. He's not told and the exertion of keeping up soon shuts him up. Back at the spot where Mike first spied the secret path, they stop to get their wind, to comprehend the thick fleece of smoke rising straight into the clear afternoon sky. Between rasping gasps Nunga relates how the fuckin' mad bastard sooled the fuckin' dog onto them and how the stupid bloody mongrel jumped in the way of the bomb — "I was only tryin' to scare it off. I hadda do somethin'." — and how the mad bastard used an axe to put the poor bloody thing out of its misery. Mike's mouth is wide open and his eyes are staring.

Nunga is about to declare the fire has forced their pursuer back into the tunnel when the mad bastard, battle axe at the ready, appears from a solid wall of furze not fifty yards away. His face and arms are scratched and bleeding, his teeth are clenched — he'd scare the living daylights out of Ned Kelly. He seems to grow a foot taller as, without wasting breath on saying anything, he immediately lunges towards them with long, swift strides. Nunga works the rifle bolt, flips off the safety and fires into the air: The man with the axe doesn't seem to notice.

"Sssshit!"

Nunga sprints after his mates, leaping and bounding down the other side of the ridge. Talk about move! They are so far ahead Nunga yells like he's already being disembowelled and they scram that much faster. They are more than half way back to the Velox before he catches up and they come to a heaving halt, too puffed for anything beyond spluttering curses at each other, one another and the heavens above. The ferrets hiss and scream and fight in their box.

The scrub fire is waning, the heavy curtain of smoke fanning out. Regaining their breath, the boys take deep chugs of their plonk and watch the Axe Man, motionless as a scarecrow on the Chinaman's Hill ridge.

"I'm never ever comin' back 'ere."

"You can say that again."

"Don't gimme the screamin' shits!" snarls Nunga, and fires off a wild, wide warning shot. "Com'n, let's get outta here before the fire brigade or some other nosy bastard comes snooping around."

An old gold moon is in the pastel dusk as Roger swings into the top end of Ponds Road and goes like a bat out of Hell to beat the gates.

The keeper has one side of the gates moving as Lanky whizzes through quick as a lizard on the wrong side of the road. "One of these days," the old gentleman consoles himself, "I'll swing 'em shut right in the silly galoot's face."

Above the silhouetted trees of the park a chattering host of starlings spin and swirl up as a fountain of snipped black flecks against the fiery glow of the western sky. Somewhere in there, way away back, is the haunt of Apple Jack. He'll be cold tonight, wherever he is.

The lake, the lake ... past the silent lake with its bellyful of cold mud and drowned babies. The water is very still tonight, a copper sheen in the gloaming.

Up a bit to Crimea Street. Houses again. The evening star, the big fat moon, velvet night is a-falling and day is done. Tyres and spokes hum-a-lum along past Rose's and into the home stretch. Street lights blink on as our boy rolls up the drive and is safe home.

Shepherds' pie for tea. Shepherds' pie served with Brussels sprouts big enough to smell like cabbages. From old Jo on down to the kids, all agree Mum's pie is real good gourmet stuff — she puts chopped onion in the mashed potato top and mixed herbs and a dash of Worchester sauce in the mince. "First, catch your shepherds!" says Dad, always. Constant demands for seconds has elevated a capacious roasting pan to the status of *the* pie dish, from which Auntie Jo, mad as The Hatter, now diligently trowels out everybody's fair serve onto the seven lined-up plates.

Fresh faced Roger, honest as the day is long, steps into the kitchen.

"And where on Earth have you been? Look at the time!"

"Me an' Mike went rabbitin' out Harcourt way. Told you last night!"

"And I told you to be home long before this." She waves the tea towel in the general direction of the clock. "I don't know how many times I've told you to be in by dark. You're worse than a dirty old Tom cat."

Dad's serve — *Splop!*

"I was in before dark. Near enough."

"Near enough isn't good enough. You've been traipsing around with that foul-mouthed guttersnipe riff-raff again I suppose. Smoking, I'll wager."

Janice's — *Thlop!*

"I'm warning you, you'd better not be drinking. I'll skin you alive if you start drinking. You can pack your bag and get out of this house if I catch you drinking. I mean it! Come here — let me smell your breath."

"Awh Mum! Come off it. Don't be so ... such a drag." He huffily stomps off up the passage towards his bedroom, and slips into the bathroom for a quick suck of the toothpaste.

"You can't fool me!" she shouts after him. "You're a scruff, a miserable little scruff."

Janice appears at the bathroom door. She pouts and has the finest line of mascara beneath her eyes. "You better give me a couple of smokes after tea if you don't want me to tell Mum."

"Yeah? An' wha'd'ya got to tell her?"

"Plenty. You know."

"Is that so? And I'll tell her you were trying to wangle smokes out of me. Tell her Nunga's been asking after you. Why's that? Been talking to him? You know, I don't get it. You try blackmail first. Why don't you just ask nicely? When have I ever held out on smokes? Maybe I should for a change — teach you to be nicer." His hand goes for her small breasts but she is too quick.

"Forget it." And she is gone.

He shrugs and dries his hands. The kids tumble in

48

to wash up for tea and Dennis turns the tap on so hard it splashes half the room and everybody in it. A gleeful little water fight ensues.

"Stop that skylarking," Mum shrieks. "Dad! *You* attend to them! They're getting too excited. You'll have to clobber them. It's that Roger — he stirs them up and eggs them on. I swear, I'll kill him."

The kids look at each other and then turn in unison to their older brother. He winks, snatches a towel and more or less wipes the puddles from the floor and the sprays from the walls. He hangs the sodden towel on the rack and quits the scene by turning out the light and slamming the door. All very hilarious, and the kids make a racket accordingly.

The smokes and matches have only just been concealed in the hollow behind the bed headboard when Dad briskly throws open Roger's bedroom door. Uh oh: time for another man-to-man chat.

"Mum says you've been drinking!" His voice is stern but his demeanour doesn't suggest annoyance.

"Awh heck! Was only a couple of swigs of sherry."

"Sherry! And where'd that spring from?"

"Mike found it. It was an old, half-full bottle in some cupboard or something. He reckons his Mum'd forgot it was there."

"That so?"

"So he sez."

"Well it don't matter if Mrs Ryan forgot it or not — it's not yours to drink. Understand?"

"Yes."

"You're bloody lucky it wasn't some kinda poison or something!"

"I reckon it just about was. Didn't feel too good after."

"Serves you right! S'pose you threw up?"

"Mike did. I just felt crook. But he drank more than me."

"Learned your lesson the hard way then." Dad allows himself a brief grin. One father is worth a hundred schoolmasters.

Roger beams. Like father, like son.

"And what about this smokin' caper again? Don't start — you'll never bloody stop."

"Awh cripes Dad! I'm not a flippin' kid, you know. I earn the money and I buy me own."

"I should bloody well hope so!"

"I always do."

"Haven't been nickin' from Charlie, have you?"

"Course not!"

"Don't even think about it because sooner or later you'll get caught. Charlie'd fire you on the spot and I'd give you such a proper hiding you wouldn't sit down for a week. And when you could sit down — I'd give you another lot as a reminder. Count on it. Got the idea?"

"Yes Dad."

"Good. Remember that and we'll get along fine. Nothing worse than a bloody thief. Get a name as a thief and nobody'll ever give you a decent job. Honesty is the best policy. Remember that."

"Honest Dad, I never pinched anything from Charlie. Well, sometimes we sample the cherries. "

Dad clears his throat and regards his honest son. "Well, that's good then. That's how it should be."

A brief lull of embarrassment. A necessary part of the proceedings.

"So! Youse didn't get any bunnies then?"

"Nawh! Them ferrets are useless. Had to dig one of 'em out of a burrow. Took us ages'n'ages. He was eating a couple a little 'uns."

"Yeah, well, they'll do that. Your uncle Laurie had ferrets when we were kids. Never liked them myself. Blood-thirsty things. Bite you quick as look at ya.

Save your money and behave yourself and I might — *might*, mind you — see about letting you have a little twenty-two one of these days.

"Yeah! Jeez, that'd be so grouse!"

"Now don't go jumping the gun — ah hahaha — so to speak. And don't say anything to Mum. You have to get a bit older here first. We'll see how you go, that's all I'm saying."

"Jeez, thanks Dad."

"All right?" And the eyebrows go up just so. "Now! Get to the table and eat your tea before it gets cold. And *don't* go getting Mum's goat. Remember, stay on the right side of her if you want to stay on the right side of me."

In the kitchen Mum glances from father to son and back again. She hands the sauce bottle to Jo and lets her question settle on Dad. Before she can ask anything he puts his arm around her shoulder and says, "Shepherd's pie, you beaut!" And then, under his breath, "Tell you a funny story later."

Jo circles the table holding the big bottle of tomato sauce. She seems distracted, as though the decision of where to place the bottle involves an overwhelming number of complex difficulties. The family watches, mesmerized. At last she reaches her place at the table, but doesn't sit because she is still preoccupied by the sauce bottle.

Dad breaks the spell. "Sit down, Jo — you're making the place look untidy."

For a nasty moment Jo looks like she's going to throw the bottle at someone, but then she bangs it down on the table by her plate and promptly sits to her meal. Everybody laughs to see such fun. Half a minute later they are all noisily digging into their tucker, just one big happy family.

The Fires

I

The first fire was in the autumn. One flawless Saturday afternoon, in the middle of the third quarter of the Tigers' first home game of the season, the volunteer brigade's siren moaned across the town. Those of us in the upper stand soon spotted the grey feather wafting into the windless, blue sky above the dry grass crest behind the State Housing Commission estate at the eastern edge of town. Within a minute it was boosted by a roiling, darker outburst, which a clutch of know-alls identified as burning furze, somewhere out along Pipers Creek Road. Players and officials held a brief, hands-on-hips conference on the field before two of our blokes left to answer the call. Snowy Sanderson stayed to play on, which was just as well because the match ended up a close run thing.

Not that the spotty crew I was with cared all that much about the bloody footy — we turned up for the laughs. Remember, this was back in those blithe days when the only organised sports inflicted upon us were strictly within school hours. In our country town, come Saturday, we were drawn to that more roisterous Life of the Mind: Talkie Bell's Saturday matinee sessions of cartoons, serials, *Three Stooges*, *Laurel and Hardy* re-runs and such. Older boys sometimes boasted of feeling up a girl in the back row, but those gropes must have to have been pretty damned quick because old Alfie, Talkie's liveried doorman, was ever-ready to flash his torch at any suspect activity.

You could go into those Saturday afternoon matinee sessions and come out after three hours into a world that'd changed. In winter it would be getting dark and rain could have come, or gone. I remember one time we came out of our warm collective fug and it had snowed. But as someone said about then, the times were a-changin'. I'm not sure when television pre-empted and ended those matinees, but by 1964 most of my cohort were seeking the promise of more penetrating experiences along the clandestine banks of the Campaspe. Looking for platy-pussies, as one comedian was want to call it.

The footy, though, could be an entertaining alternative, with the real sport being off rather than on the showground oval. As it happened, the visitors for that first home game were a strong Bendigo team with four or five busloads of supporters. It was one of those small town things: incipient civic pride and the expectation of a big turnout combined to generate enough momentum to entice even us incorrigibles to join the herd. Besides, we could count on someone's older brother slipping us a bottle of beer to swig behind the stables. There was, too, the firm prospect of ogling the visiting players' girlfriends.

Anyway, that first fire was easily dealt with. The dark smoke was not gorse, but half a drum of Christ-only-knows-what Ted Watson had left in a derelict hayshed on his back paddock. Standing clear in a flat field of overgrazed pale stubble, the shed was left to burn while the brigade circled to contain the slow crackle of the fire's perimeter. By the time the mop up was over a near full moon was coolly rising over a two-acre black sphere centred on a collapsed heap of charred timber and buckled corrugated iron.

It was as plain as the nose on your face. Everybody agreed, one look was enough to know — that fire had been deliberately lit.

Doc "Just-a-splash" Connell, ensconced Golf Club President, phoned in the alarm from the club's rooms; from the members' bar, to be precise. The Doc and a few fellow sportsmen were refreshing themselves, over a discussion about the state of the road from Malmsbury to Daylesford, when a player rushed in to report the sudden appearance of smoke the other side of Baynton Road. Being one of those on the Doc's list for tournament caddying or ball-spotting, I could just see him, generous measure of Dewar's in hand, raising a bristling eyebrow at the noisy interruption.

Of course, none of the golfers saw who or what started the fire. No suspicious cars were seen along either of the nearby roads. Ted Watson and his two boys were at the footy after dropping Mrs Watson off at her sister's for the afternoon, so they were no help. Someone saw Brian Jenkins, his little brother and their cousin, that oldest Simpson kid who was always getting the cuts at school, working their ferrets and dog along the stony rise further up Baynton Road, but that young gang indignantly denied having anything to do with the fire. They admitted seeing the shed burning before the brigade arrived, but insisted they had not noticed anyone in the vicinity. Sergeant McPherson, our boss copper, eventually let it be known he believed them.

Not that the Sergeant ruled out other wayward brats. He noted the configuration of hedges, roadside ditches and the general lie of the land allowed someone heading back to the Boundary Road side of town to quickly cover a lot of ground without being seen. In the absence of anyone to blame, the town's judgement drifted towards half finished sentences about unnamed kids playing with matches.

Then again, who knows, it could have been a carload of bodgies up from Melbourne. Some of those yobbos seemed to think they had a perfect right to clamour over fences and wander onto other people's land to pick or kick mushrooms. They went into paddocks containing sheep and one lot had even been caught doing a bit of shooting. Such people were as careless about closing gates as they were about where they flicked their cigarette butts. You only needed to take one look to see most of them were silly enough to throw a lighted match on a dare. My Mum said they were Bad Eggs; and, believe you me, she knew a Bad Egg when she saw one.

It was only after subsequent events that people looked back and started calling the destruction of Watson's shed "the first fire". At first, it was just one of those things people talk about for a few days, until some larrikin got into a punch-up outside the Shamrock or rolled a car or was party to a hasty wedding announcement. At the time, the big thing about that fire was the fact it disrupted the footy. It wasn't in town, there was no real damage — not memorable.

The kind of fire people remembered, one that had quickly become a town legend (The Big Fire), was the blaze that had torn through Wilfred Scriber's Furniture and Electrical Appliance Emporium one night a couple of winters back. People talk about roaring fires — well, let me tell you, that was a bloody ripper. You had to see it, *hear* it, to believe it. Imagine: burning, an old, wooden warehouse filled with varnished wardrobes, solid oak tables, pine-frame sofas and just about every flammable substance known to civilization; all under Oregon beams and resting on floorboards waxed and polished for going on eighty years. My, oh my, Wilfred's store certainly burned hard and fast.

Happening on a Wednesday night, and because Wilfred's Emporium was opposite the town hall, our picture theatre, quite a few of us had a grand view. I can't remember what was on the bill that night — a Western or Horror more than likely — but a sizable proportion of the town's male population were there. Anyway, Talkie stopped the show, turned on the lights and advised patrons with cars parked out the front to shift them because there was a fire across the street. So we all shoved our way out onto the front steps to witness the brigade gamely holding the ferocious flames from spreading to the neighbouring buildings, which, fortunately, were stone and brick with slate rooves. You could feel the heat on your face as soon as you came out of the theatre.

Just as soon as we were all assembled, Wilfred's two-tone blue Customline came barrelling up and skidded to a stop in the middle of Mollison Street. The motor running, he jumped out in his daggy dressing gown and leather slippers and rushed about putting on quite an act, literally wringing his hands and clutching his head. Never underestimate the use of theatrics. In hindsight, I have to say, old Wilfred's performance was very impressive. Sergeant McPherson, hands in his pockets as he contemplated the show, directed someone to move the car out of harm's way. A few blokes led Wilfred over to sit on the hall's steps and set about settling him down. I remember looking down and seeing the fire reflecting off his bald pate.

Many later remarked in a conspiratorial tone that you could smell the petrol. You couldn't actually smell petrol, obviously, but people felt obliged to say something. And those who heard the remark, felt obliged to repeat it.

At its height, the Emporium fire really was an absolute pearler. But with the arrival of the Woodend brigade's engine to work the back of the building, the balance shifted and the high drama was over. Even so, although matters were down to the dousing stage when Alfie finally came out to announce Talkie was about to restart the film, many patrons hesitated and lingered before returning to the shelter and fold of the Technicolor trance.

Then, after the spectacle of the fire itself, there followed long and tangled strings of gossip, enough to entertain the town for months. In the end we all knew, without quite knowing how we knew, that Wilfred arranged the job for the insurance. Sly old bastard got away with it, too. Clean away. Retired to North Queensland. Funny thing was, years later, a decade or more, a story seeped back from the Sunshine State about a block of holiday apartments owned by Wilfred's son having to be knocked down after a suspicious fire. Small world.

But that's another story. The thing about Wilfred's fire was that there were some in the town, not everyone, who came to think it may have somehow been the genesis of what came later. Their idea — they called it their *theory* — which was supported by a very interesting article about pyromania in an old copy of *Parade* magazine available for the waiting customers in Mr Firth's barbershop, was that someone stood there that night in the crowd outside the picture theatre and watched the mighty conflagration in such awe and rapture that, sooner or later, they simply had to seek it again.

Perhaps they were right. Stranger things have happened.

II

The second fire was at the Kyneton District High School. The block of classrooms next to the old saleyards went up in the middle of the night, after the moon had set — a winter's night of high, thin cloud. I had a great view from my bedroom window, over our back fence, across an open paddock, the tennis courts and the school oval. Once the fire took hold it could be seen all over town, lighting the underbelly of angry smoke furling up into the darkness. The ruby glow could be seen from farms in the surrounding countryside. In the frosty stillness, many of us living closer to the school also heard the snap, crackle, pop and, especially, the *boom*-TZ*Ah*SCH of shattering windows. Yes, there was a lot of glass in those old 1950s standard plan classroom blocks. Tar paper, too, for insulation; and that stuff burned with its own particular insistence.

It was a four-room job: two rooms either side of a wide, locker-lined corridor down the guts. With big double doors at the top of a few steps at either end, the thing was mounted on wooden piles with the under space enclosed by creosoted slats. Some of those had been jemmied off, broken and shoved back under the building. Throw in scrunched sheets of newspaper, splash about petrol or kero and it was just one scratch of a match for ... *whoosh*!

That, anyway, was what the expert detectives from Melbourne determined as the *modus operandi*. They were from the Arson Squad and we had to concede such specialists ought to know what they were talking about. The three of them wore three-piece suits (no overalls!) and arrived soon after first light in a dark blue Ford Falcon station wagon, last year's model. Sergeant McPherson had his two young constables keep us kids and some nosy parents at bay while he and Tom Wedge, our *basso profondo* Fire Chief, showed the city-slickers around the still smouldering ruin. One of them took photographs while the others walked up and down, nudging this and that with the sides of their shiny shoes (Tom Wedge wore *his* gumboots), squatted and peered, stood and conferred in a professional manner, nodded and examined something else, and then wandered back and forth some more with their hands in their pockets. The sky was blue, the air was crisp and the sun silvered the dewy cobwebs on the broad, mown meadow that did as our sports field.

As instructed, we stood back. Affecting nonchalant stances with hands in pockets, the boys hung around beside their bike shed; the girls clustered near the canteen, the sleeves of their grey pullovers pulled down over clenched fists. We observed and commented on the rows of aluminium window frames rather neatly dropped either side of the building, and noted how far out from the fire the playground asphalt had bubbled. We townies were quizzed by every busload of country kids as they arrived to get the proverbial eyeful. We speculated as to whether anything could be salvaged from the blackened banks of lockers that lay like the charred spine of a burnt animal carcass. Some of the first form girls, whose lockers they were, bleated and snivelled a bit, but the rest of us just calmly watched the cops go about their business — aware that they were also quietly sizing us up. Clean shaven men in their late thirties, they wore dapper hats and, as we all noticed and McPherson remarked to a small group of confidants in the back bar of the Royal that evening, the blighters all smoked like chimneys. The other snippet McPherson told his coterie was that none of The Squad used anything so ordinary as a box of Redheads. They all had flip-top Ronson lighters, shiny new brass ones upon which their names were engraved. "Don't ask me," McPherson warned before the question was put to him.

The Arson Squad ... yes, well, naturally, there were jokes (predictable). Pretty well all of the boys of the lower school and the coarser adults of the town were overwhelmed and rendered near breathless by their own side-splitting wit, most of which hinged on that delightful word: "bugger".

Anyway, to cut to the chase, just as Stiffy Glover, Deputy Head, blows his whistle and orders those left without a classroom to take themselves off to the assembly hall, McPherson shepherds his colleagues away for a tour of the buyers' inspection walkways atop the maze of the saleyards' aged timber enclosures. On most sale days business was conducted in the pens closest to the stock agent's office, well away from the school; especially when it was hot with the wind in the wrong direction. But on busy days some stock — cattle, sheep and the occasional lot of pigs — was held in a section of the yards nearer but not quite next to the school. This had not happened for a while, so the place had not been hosed out and quite a bit of rubbish had built up, including the school smoking brigade's discarded butts and cigarette packets. If the cops, their own fags adroitly hanging off their bottom lips, found anything of significance they didn't let on. Even so, it was generally reckoned the saleyards had been the arsonist's most likely escape route. Personally, I always thought that was a conclusion reached by intuition rather than logic. The arsonist ...

There, you see, there you have it: the arsonist. Someone had been designated the role; a role, as the philosophers say, with agency. Now there was a presence lurking behind the fire. Someone planned it. Someone did it. A specific someone who was probably one of us. Someone else, too, must know or suspect something. It was immediately taken for granted that the culprit had to be some bloody kid, a current or former student, some damned juvenile delinquent engaging in arrant vandalism. People always go for the obvious.

Nine times out of ten they are right.

Mum got me alone that evening and for the time it took her to smoke a contemplative Craven "A" engaged me in a conversation aimed at discovering what, exactly, I had heard. It was hard to tell whether she was relieved or disappointed when I told her the kids at school knew no more than anybody else in the town. After a long, hard look to make double sure I wasn't hiding anything, I was told to keep my ear to the ground and if I did hear anything to immediately report to her and Dad.

This is where I should mention that though our families didn't socialize beyond pleasantries in the street, Dad and Sergeant McPherson were fairly matey. As the district's Lands Department Inspector, my father had a steady stream of minor official business with the Sergeant. They were fellow members of the local branch of the Returned Sailors' Soldiers' and Airmen's Imperial League of Australia and marched together on Anzac Day. They were also both members of the Lodge. When required, they knew where to apply a quiet word to get things done behind the scenes.

Mum's quiet word was still buzzing in my ears when everybody got the official version at the school the following morning. Kyneton High had a really good hall, complete with a projection box and a raised stage with proscenium arch. When the school was built back in the 1920s there was plenty of room for everyone, but with the baby boom and even the farm kids staying at school for a year or so longer, the hall had only space enough for half the roll. So we had split sittings for indoor assemblies on days when the weather prevented the usual sprawling line ups on the netball courts. I remember — God's Truth! — mornings when the fog was so thick we had to go inside just to see who was who.

Even a half school assembly in the hall required a bit of push and shove with some of us having to stand at the back. But no matter how tight the fit, the girls-on-the-right, boys-on-the-left rule was always strictly enforced. This didn't stop Phillip Baron from sitting close to the aisle well back from the stage and, for the discernment and delectation of Lorraine Taylor and her companions, providing a discreet flash of his engorged knob. "Sharing a private moment," he used to call it. He had this hilarious trick of draping his school cap over his erect member — then flexing it to make the cap waggle back and forth. Thinking about that stunt now, and considering how often he did it, it's a real wonder he got away with it. Last I heard of Phillip, sometime in the late 1970s, he was reading the news on an Adelaide radio station. Probably a good thing he never worked on television.

But on the day with which we are concerned beastly Phil kept his cock in his pants and it wasn't the weather that put us in the hall. Although that morning was the same frosty fine as the previous one, Porkie Veal understood the hall's excellent acoustics facilitated a more modulated tone of sombre address than could ever be achieved in braying oneself hoarse through a megaphone in the open air. After the lower school had their talk, we upper school mob filed in for our more serious lecture.

His magnificent bulk enhanced by his voluminous academic gown (his tasselled mortar board was a treat only ever donned for very special occasions) and hitching his thumbs into his waist coat, our enormous headmaster shone his broad, florid face over his attentive charges. He let a deep silence flow into every corner of the hall before he drew a heavy breath and stared over our heads to address the dark eye of the projection box. "I wish we could have welcomed Sergeant McPherson in more propitious circumstances ..." He trailed off, lost for words.

It was, naturally, all show. We all knew Porkie was no slug when it came to orotund rhetoric and Thespian sorcery. But other than a few words on the significant financial cost and disruption caused by the wanton, shameful act we had "witnessed", Porkie left the policeman to deliver the message. Plainly put: if any of us knew anything about this "serious criminal matter", the next twenty-four hours was the time to say so.

Sergeant McPherson's avuncular routine was polished; a measured, reasonable explanation of how things stood. It wasn't as if any of us were necessarily under suspicion, you understand, but one of us might know something to fill a gap or confirm a detail of the wider investigation. A police investigation, he told us, was like doing a jigsaw puzzle that had pieces missing. Had any of us, for example, been spoken to by or seen any strangers near the school in the last few weeks? Think back. Noticed any strange cars? Or perhaps we'd heard something "odd" ... at school, on the bus, or maybe from older boys talking on a street corner. We should also realise that whoever lit this fire could go on to light another. In fact, they probably would. That's why such people were dangerous. People could be hurt. Or worse.

The policeman paused to let that stark truth sink in before expressing his regret at having to say it, but there was a strong possibility some of us "in this very hall" actually knew the culprit. Not that he was saying we knew the culprit was the culprit, if you follow me, but when all was revealed some of us may have the unpleasant experience of discovering the culprit was "closer to home" than we would like. This was a time, he told us, when we had to put personal loyalties aside — "And, believe me, I understand, that can be a very hard thing to do." — and act upon, fulfil our duty to the community. So, if we thought we knew something we should talk it over with our parents or teachers and the Sergeant or one of his constables would then talk to us "in confidence".

Some things, he said as a matter-of-fact aside, were already known. Finally, a glint of the blade was shown when he reminded us that to knowingly withhold information was in itself an offence. The words "complicity" and "accomplice" were uttered.

We all stared at Sergeant McPherson's shiny buttons. Nobody dropped a pin.

Porkie cleared his throat and stepped forward. After contemplating the upturned faces, the motionless mass of blemished innocence before him, the headmaster quietly dismissed us to our classes. Solemnly taking McPherson's elbow, he politely ushered the policeman off stage and out of sight into the wing behind Miss Poole's upright piano.

I'd been sitting next to Morrie White, a kid bussed up from Gisborne, and even before we were out of the hall he was giggling at the idea of writing a note implicating Fluffy Seale, the poncy Arts and Crafts teacher.

I have to admit, it seemed like a good idea at the time.

My best mate at that wayward stage of my life was a kid named Ronnie Scott. Scottie wore glasses, didn't smoke and was a bit of a weed, but he was game for anything. One lunchtime in our last year at primary school he snuck up a painter's ladder, somehow scrambled up the steep pitch of the slate roof past the chimney and, arms outstretched, walked back and forth on one of the high ridges traversing the building. Such athleticism was surprising from a buck-toothed, weakling who, even then, openly shunned Sport. But Scottie was full of surprises. When ordered down by Hogan, our outwardly calm but red-faced senior teacher, Ronald Alexander Scott did another defiant lap and showed off with several deep, slow bows as his finale. Ten minutes later, in front of the class, he took six of the best from Hogan's zinging leather strap without flinching.

We had always been friendly, but over the year or so before the fires our growing mutual interest in science fiction, paranormal phenomena, UFOs and chemistry experiments had us spending a lot of our weekends together. If you cut across the paddock behind the tennis courts, our homes were only minutes apart. Mostly I went to his place because, being an only child, Scottie had his own room and his mother always had a piece of good cake at the ready. We listened to his father's short-wave radio, yarned and borrowed or swapped books, magazines and certain comics. I had all the Classics Illustrated titles of Jules Verne and H.G. Wells, and Scottie introduced me to the writings of Lobsang Rampa. *The Third Eye* and *Doctor from Lhasa* — What more can I say? — those books revealed the philosophical Life of the Mind to many a gormless youth and I was one of them. It was heady stuff. Only the metaphysics of Pauline Sanderson's swelling breasts and lengthening thighs could distract us from the mechanics of astral travel. Unlike most kids of our age in that time and place, rather than racing about the streets on our bikes, we preferred to walk and talk and philosophize. Besides, our speculative comings and goings often took us past the back of the tennis courts to observe Pauline's lithe moves.

But Pauline's winning serve was not on our minds as Scottie and I did our lunchtime circuit of the sports field the day of that extraordinary assembly. Even then, a day and a half after the blaze, you could still smell some residue in the air, some ghost of the smoke. I had just told him of Morrie's idea of dobbing Fluffy Seale when Scottie suddenly came out with: "We oughta make ourselves a proper wee-jar board, a fair dinkum wooden one, and set it up an' do it all proper and ask it who burnt the bloody classrooms. Coz, you know, some joker bloody well did it! Right!?"

He was right. Somebody did it. You couldn't argue with that.

"But, listen," I ventured, "suppose we get a name, we'd still have to, you know ... we'd have to have some kind of *actual* proof."

"We'll find it," he shot back with the absolute confidence of a clear-eyed realist. "If you know where to look, you'll find your proof."

Right again!

"Seriously," he added, "like they say, where there's smoke there's fire."

If I was about to laugh he cut me off with, "I was thinking." He looked about to make sure nobody could overhear. "Just look at that," he glanced toward the burnt out ruin. "A fire like that takes the evidence. Those cops can't be sure how it started. Suppose someone left something in one of the desks. Just suppose. Really, from what's left, how would they ever know?"

"What? A bomb?!"

"Technically speaking, an incendiary device. Perhaps

as simple as gunpowder mixed with phosphorus. With a timer."

"A timer? What ... an alarm clock?"

Scottie sighed and shook his head at my sophisticated joke. Then, squinting like he did when tying a slip knot, he raised his right index finger. "I betcha," he chirped, "I betcha anything you like there's something in that big Yankee chemistry book in the library."

"I betcha you're right!"

Without another word we were running across the oval, all the way up the slope to the main building before slowing to a fast walk along the corridor to the school library. Panting, we glanced at the clock as we entered: ten minutes before the bell.

Scottie headed straight for the science shelves but even before he got there we both saw the book we were after on the back corner table. It was open before Alan Baker, who was busy taking notes. I met Scottie's widened eyes and raised my eyebrows. We had been in this situation before — the school library held single copies of certain books in which Scottie and Alan shared a competitive interest and that competition was not friendly.

There are always at least two sides to every story, but we felt Alan was the cause of the antagonism. He was such a moody bastard, one of those pricks who keep to themselves for the simple but compelling reason they just don't have a lot of friends — mind you, he'd only come to our school the year before when his father was transferred from somewhere in New South Wales to manage our town's branch of the Commonwealth Bank. A year ahead of us, Alan was a big, solid bloke with sandy-reddish hair and thin lips. He had not so much as glanced up when, with us still a few paces away, he loudly slammed shut the hefty vol, turned his notebook face down and locked his yellow eyes on us with an irritable, threatening, "What?" The glare he gave Scottie stopped us in our tracks.

Scottie raised a finger as though to say something important, thought better of it and gave Alan the cheeky cheesy grin. "Nuffin'," he said. "Just wondering when ..." he pointed at the chemistry book.

Alan didn't blink.

Scottie held his ground and Alan's stare for a duration and then shrugged. "OK. We'll come back later," he said, and backed off.

I thought: I'll cut this prick down to size.

Every other kid in the room relished our retreat. Even silly old Chook Fowler, the ninny librarian, wobbled her narrow head in silent mirth.

"Couldn't see what he was looking at," Scottie sighed when we were back in the corridor and the library door had banged shut behind our backs. "I guess you were too far away."

"The book was open," I told him, "about the three-quarter mark."

He stopped, his eyes fixed on the floor. Delicately pinching together the fingers and thumb of each hand, Scottie lightly touched their tips to either side of his forehead, as though feeling for the buds of tiny devil's horns. He closed his eyes in pained concentration and slowly drew in a deep breath. He held it, perfectly still, for at least five seconds. Suddenly his eyes opened wide, his arms flew up, fingers outstretched, and he whispered, "He's up to something!"

It was on the tip of my tongue to suggest Alan may have been acting on the same investigative curiosity motivating Scottie when he blurted: "Why'd he hide it? He is *definitely* up to something. I just know he is. He's always at that book. Or hanging around the science room. He's the one who's been nicking the test tubes, you know."

"Why's he need to do that? His Old Man's got plenty dough!" Town joke: Mr Baker being a bank manager and all.

"Yeah, right," Scottie impatiently waved the lazy jest aside. "You know, Baker gets those electronics magazines. Ma Wilson keeps them for him behind the counter. Collects them Saturday mornings."

"You're right!"

"And see, *see!*, Saturdee morning, when everybody's up and down the main street muckin' about — Baker's always on his own! And always scribbling something in that notebook he carts round. Walks right past you like you don't exist. Snooty bastard."

"Remember, everybody thought he was the one chucking penny bungers on people's rooves last year?"

"On his own! See what I mean! Who does that sorta stuff on their own? I mean, that's the sorta stuff you do with your mates. Like when me an' Maxie Symonds put that dead snake in bloody old Hogan's letterbox. But Alan fricken Baker ... who's he ever with?"

"Maybe he was with someone. I mean, they never got caught."

"Pull the other one! Really, who'd you reckon that was? His big sister? Mad Marlene? She's cracked! Silly as a two-bob watch. You know, it's true what they say, they packed her off to boarding school coz she beat up her mother."

"So they say."

"Anyway — known cracker thrower — you have to think it was him got something the size of a thrupp-nee bunger down the Sullivans' chimney. Fluck shot. Went off halfway down. They were cleaning up soot and crap in their lounge room for days AND ... "

" ... it damaged the chimney!" we said together.

"And ..." Scottie dropped his voice, "I reckon he made that big bastard himself."

"You reckon?"

"I reckon he took a bought one and souped up the charge."

"You reckon?"

"Not that hard to do."

"True."

It all fitted. We fell into step and quickened our pace.

As with so much else to do with those fires, Scottie was barking up the wrong tree. One cold and windy twilight, my father's prized Carl Zeiss binoculars swinging on their leather strap around my scrawny neck, we actually climbed a big, swishing pine at the back corner of the primary school. Oh, the antics of having a bit of fun and honing your surveillance skills — although picking open Alan Baker's locker without having figured out how to relock it wasn't exactly James Bond.

Yes, we got carried away with spying on Alan and one thing led to another and then before we knew it we had an awkward situation on our hands. But, alas, is that not an all too common story? Don't tell me it hasn't happened to you.

I can hand-on-heart swear I never said anything to anyone concerning Scottie's suspicion that Alan somehow had an ingenious hand in the classrooms fire. Well, when I say *never*, I mean before everything blew up in our faces and we were confronted by all the head shaking of fuming parents and the judgement of Porkie Veal. Then, no choice, I had to come clean and own up.

More or less. I never did tell Dad we'd borrowed his field glasses.

The problem was Scottie couldn't keep his trap shut. Couldn't do it. He just had to talk about whatever was buzzing around in his head. Who knows what he said? I don't know who he spoke to. He didn't know himself. Christ, he talked to himself aloud and didn't know it. He might have let slip something to Maxie or some other kid in his science class. Or perhaps it had been one lunch time in the library when I wasn't there to absorb the prattle. Or ... you know, as the kids say in these past-modern days — Whatever!

What was never in doubt was how it came before Porkie. Alan's father, a pillar of the community (etc.), personally made an appointment and visited the school to inform the headmaster of what was going on — he gave names of at least two kids for Porkie to talk to — and went so far as to politely suggest that if the matter was not addressed he would, regretfully, have to lodge a complaint directly to the Education Department.

There was justice in the fact that Scottie took the brunt of the head shaking and general displeasure, but there was enough to go around and a good dollop was directed at yours truly, the sneaky accomplice.

What surprised and worried us was that the supposedly friendless Alan found a couple of kids to enthusiastically dob us, to say they'd seen us at his locker. I was the lookout but, so help me, could honestly swear to Scottie that I really couldn't figure who saw us in the seniors' locker room. We were left guessing. Alan Baker was not just clever, he was damned cunning.

Just for the record: we found nothing out of the ordinary in his locker; fact is, it would have got the blue ribbon for tidiness. I remember, I said to Scottie, it was like he expected us.

The thunderclap summons to Porkie's office and the ensuing ear-burning litany of maternal disappointment at home came two weeks to the day after the fire. I have to say, standing before the judicial bench of the headmaster's big desk, Scottie put on a good performance — bravura, as they say. I even thought I saw Porkie's jowls quiver in wonderment at the sheer audacity of what he was being served. What Porkie usually heard in response to his "What have you got to say for yourself?" was either a huffy "He started it!" or a mumbled "Nuffin', Sir." But Scottie took a deep breath and was off like the proverbial hare.

Basically, he told the truth. As he saw it. He had been honestly — mistakenly perhaps, but honestly — investigating how a fire, like the one recently seen, could be started using a chemical process that took several hours to mature and ignite flammable material. Most of the basic information, he claimed, was available in a book in the school library — it was there (he pointed through the appropriate wall) for all to see in black and white — in a book Alan Baker had consulted many times! When Scottie started to elaborate the chemistry involved Porkie cleared his throat and reminded him that he had said "most of the basic information". "So I presume," he went on, "your bomb could not be made, even if all the materials were available, just from what appears in that textbook." Scottie conceded that was so but immediately countered by saying Alan knew a lot about chemistry and it was well-known he had previously made his own fireworks. In fact ...

Porkie stopped him with an impatient flick of his fingers, swivelled his big Captain's chair, leaned back and stretched out his heavy legs. He seemed to be addressing the toes of his beautifully polished black shoes as he cryptically remarked that if one intended to fill the hole by using the same shovel with which you dug it, it would be a good idea to first get out of that hole. Ignorant tittle-tattle about the fire was a silliness he could ultimately forgive, but breaking into another student's locker was something far too serious to leave unpunished. He sat up straight behind his desk, adjusted his wire-rimmed spectacles, folded his hands before him and pronounced, "The school will not tolerate it." He fixed Scottie with his blue eyes, startlingly magnified by his glasses, "I *shall* not tolerate it."

"So," he rumbled at me, "you were the lookout?"

"Yes, Sir."

"That didn't go to plan, did it?"

"No, Sir."

"And what else have you to add to this sorry tale?"

"Nuffin', Sir." I knew my lines. "Did the wrong thing, Sir."

"You did. It's a good thing nothing was missing. Or has been *said* to be missing."

He rubbed his chubby, dimpled chin while he let the last comment sink in before he leaned back and informed us we would both be apologising to Alan Baker. The instruction was hardly out of his mouth when he reached forward to grab and vigorously shake the small hand bell on his desk. The office door was immediately swung open by Minnie Mouse, Porkie's secretary, and in stepped the aggrieved parties, Alan and his father.

Porkie rose and attentively directed Mr Baker to a chair facing us beside his desk. Alan stood beside his father. Porkie straightened his gown and resumed his seat. Scottie and me were, as required by the age-old script of tradition, standing facing them, our hands clasped behind our backs.

Everybody looked at Scottie. Even I, shifting my weight and lowering my eyes, stole a glance. He looked perplexed, like he had missed his cue in a play. For a horrible moment I thought he was going to stuff up and say something really stupid. I sensed Porkie was about to clear his throat in warning, but Scottie got in first and, sporting his worst

Bugs Bunny grin, delivered his apologies to Alan *and* his father *and* Porkie with honeyed sincerity.

Messrs Baker and Veal exchanged nods of satisfaction. Unseen by his elders, Alan slashed a smirk at us.

Porkie levelled his gaze on me. My turn.

"I'm sorry, too," I mumbled. "We didn't mean it."

I guessed Porkie was considering asking me to clarify that last bit, so I shuffled and looked confused and he took the executive decision to wind up that part of proceedings. He stood and pointed to where Scottie and I were to stand and wait out of the way as the Bakers, *pater et filius*, took their leave.

Porkie placed us so Minnie could keep her beady eyes on us while he was giving the placated bank manager the big "all-good" handshake on the front steps. This didn't stop Scottie squeezing "We didn't mean it! Good one!" out of the side of his mouth.

We were still struggling to suppress the laughter ballooning within us when Porkie came back and amiably ambled by us to take off his gown and — nice old duffer — carefully fold and drape it over the back of his chair. He then casually adjusted his sprung steel shirt-sleeve holders and picked up the leather strap we had not noticed furled like a sleeping snake in his book case. Without another word, without even bothering with the ritual of limbering up, he gave both of us six of the best to be going on with. Oddly, we hadn't expected that. I assume age and size may have slowed him, but Porkie's technique of giving the cuts remained pretty damned lethal.

"This is not yet finished," he said, sweet and mild as you like, and told us to return after classes to collect the letters he was about to write to our parents.

Apart from the noisy dramatics of Mum waving Porkie's two-line letter in my face whenever I looked sideways, the main result for me was being kept home on the weekends. The letter itself was hardly Exhibit A in a criminal case. Porkie merely informed my parents he had administered corporal punishment and asked them to contact him at their earliest possible convenience. So Dad phoned and got the story with the friendly suggestion it might be better for Scottie and I not to see each other for a while. The whole thing was handled without fuss, in the manner of gents with more important things on their minds.

Scottie was not so lucky. His mother made a spectacle of herself by tarting up and personally visiting Mr Veal to plead young Ronald's case and generally assure the headmaster it was all just boyish high jinx. The pity of it was she dressed like she was off to see the 1954 Melbourne Cup — and her visit was during the lunch hour, so half the school saw her strut in and all of the school saw her traipse away. Scottie did his best not to show his embarrassment, but he was bloody mortified.

Over the following week or so there were a few remarks about the honour of getting the cuts from Porkie, but things settled down soon enough with a punch-up behind the bike shed and Phillip Baron flashing the full length of his glowing prong for the approval of a table of fourth form girls in the canteen. It was not until a fortnight later, at the end of the last day before the term holiday, that Scottie opened his locker to find a bunger the size of and as red as Phillip's dick. The fuse was snipped off close, down to two seconds' worth if you were quick and lucky.

Rather than even attempting to cope with four squabbling boys for two weeks of term holidays, mother gladly farmed us out to relatives. I had cousins all over the state and swaps were routine — one or two of us out of the way, replaced by visitors on their best behaviour, vastly improved household dynamics and mother's temper. It had already been arranged for two of my younger brothers to be traded for the twins from Euroa, a pair of nine-year-old girls my mother adored. I had been going to stay home in Kyneton, Dad had as good as promised to take Scottie and me out on his rounds, but after the chat with Porkie other arrangements were made. It would be bad form for Dad to be seen arming us with .22 rifles and roaming over grassy hillsides shooting rabbits. Anyway, you guessed it, I was packed off to Melbourne to stay with my dear old great aunt in Coburg.

Bessie had no grandchildren: one son died in the war and the other, Arthur, was a middle-aged bachelor living in Sydney. Great uncle Bill died when I was a baby and Bessie had made my brothers and me her de facto grandchildren. She kept house for her spinster sister, Annie (a lingerie saleswoman), and their bachelor brother, Jim (a tram conductor), both of whom were away all day (and sometimes weekends), so Bessie was mostly on her own. I'd had holiday stays with her from before I could remember and knew her suburb and all its back lanes like a local. Her roomy weatherboard house with its deep backyard was a short walk from Moreland train station and only a block west of Sydney Road and the trams, so getting to and from the city was not a problem — especially for a fifteen-year old with an extra thirty shillings holiday money burning a hole in his pocket.

I could part with the little brown ten-bob note with not much more than a blink, but breaking and letting go of that magnificent one-pound note was best done for some special purchase or occasion. Purchase and occasion came together when Scottie and I had a spree in the magicians' supply shop in a basement off Flinders Lane. Yes, unbeknown to anyone other than us, Scottie's parents also had the bright idea of sending him off to

Melbourne for the holidays. His working uncle and dizzy-busy aunt lived out at Mount Waverley, a half hour train ride from Flinders Street, and were as trusting of Scottie as Bessie was of me. We had quietly arranged matters to the minute before we left Kyneton.

At the magic shop we admired a magnificent silk-lined cape. The bloke let us try it on and swish it about a bit, even though it was obviously light years out of our price range. I bought a pack of marked cards; Scottie got a bottle of flash powder, some fuse paper and a neat little whoopee cushion. We splurged a bit more of our cash with celebratory milkshakes and cheese pastries in the Greek cafe across the lane. We managed to keep the rest of our money in our pockets that day, but we did loiter in Myers' philatelic department and check out the sci-fi shelves of a big second-hand bookshop.

Along the way we talked a bit about Alan Baker putting that giant firecracker into Scottie's locker. I agreed with Scottie's idea that Alan must have a master key — picking a lock with a safety pin was one thing, but relocking it was altogether another. Although I said Scottie should have reported it straightaway, I also saw that having removed and taken the thing home it was now better to shut up. "I reckon," he nodded darkly, "the bastard expected me to report it so he could deny it and force me to prove different which, you know, would be ... difficult."

"Yes," I agreed. "But, I dunno, why would he have put it there?"

"Provocation!" he snapped. "It was! We're gunna have to be on our guard. This is really some kind of stirred up what's-its' nest."

"Hornets?"

"Wasps. He just better remember, you know, two can play at this game."

"What'd'ya mean?"

"Well, I mean ... What I mean is ... He'll keep."

With hindsight it's easy to say I should have diverted poor old Scottie. But, honestly, although it was easy to talk him into something, trying to talk him out of something when he got that glassy-eyed raver look often as not only put more wind in his sails. I didn't ask and Scottie didn't say, so Alan wasn't mentioned when we got together again in the city the following week. It was one of those early September days when Melbourne has three seasons in one day. We dodged the late morning showers at an hour show of cartoons and newsreels in a small picture theatre at the bottom of Elizabeth Street, then caught a tram up to the Queen Victoria market, where we loutishly dined on fatty sticks of very garlicky kabana while unsuccessfully searching for the bloke said to sell live carpet snakes at ten shillings a foot. After that adventure we headed across to the top of Swanston Street to give the museum the once over. We'd both been there before, of course, but separately; together, we examined the articulated boa constrictor skeleton while surreptitiously gawking at a pair of sophisticated city girls wearing tight cashmere sweaters and disturbingly short skirts. I dared Scottie to do a Phillip Baron flash. I tell you — he thought about it. It was a great day. I remember it fondly.

It's odd, the funny things that stick in memory for no apparent reason. I remember getting off the train at Moreland station. I was a little later than I should have been getting home to Bessie's and it was already getting dark. Bare bulbs under shades like dinner plates lit the station's name signs either end of the platform. Beyond a mesh fence, in a small park, you can see a mature date palm silhouetted against the cold, apricot gloaming. I stood there studying that sky for a minute while the flock of tired shop assistants and office workers returning from the city filed past the ticket collector. A burst of starlings whooshed overhead, whirled and flurried around the head of the palm, then darted off towards the Brunswick tram sheds.

A young man stood on the opposite platform smoking a cigarette and, like me, contemplating the heavens. He was wearing a white lab coat — I guess he worked at the Sacred Heart Hospital just to the west along Moreland Road. As my train rattled off up the line towards Coburg, a city-bound one passed it coming down. Its headlight flowed down the rails as molten gold; and the big pantograph, up there like a quiff on the front carriage, threw the occasional blue spark from the overhead wires. Just before the train arrived the man in the lab coat flicked the glowing butt of his cigarette onto the tracks. I saw it arc and land in a small burst of sparks.

The following day was my last but one in Melbourne and I'd promised Bessie I'd go with her to the superette and butcher up near the Bell Street-Sydney Road intersection. Don't get me wrong, helping her with the shopping was not a chore. Bessie was always good company and I enjoyed tagging along as she did her rounds. Everybody knew and made a fuss of the stout old lady in the long black coat with her string bags and the old-style canvas shopping trolley. In the superette I fetched what Bessie could not easily reach and read the fine print on the labels. When the burly butcher added up his bill he rounded back the total by knocking off the pence, and then threw in an extra couple of sausages "to help feed a growing lad". We were home — shoes off, aarhh, my poor old aching feet ... a glass of cold water — and unpacked by midday. Bessie made me lunch by frying a couple of those sausages to go with a small tin of baked beans on toast. She, regular as clockwork, treated herself to lots of butter and jam on fresh white bread.

The news came over the wireless while we were doing the dishes. After the main stories there was a short report of a former Education Department employee being caught red-handed setting fire to Broadford High. The police said the man was being questioned, adding that a recent fire at Kyneton District High was still being investigated. Broadford, like Kyneton, was about an hour's drive from Melbourne.

Bessie and I looked at each other. "They ought to give mongrels like that a jolly good flogging," she said, gentle as a lamb.

I wondered, concentrating on drying the ferrule of the knife, whether she knew Porkie had jolly well given me the cuts?

Further details were published in the next morning's papers. Like everybody else in my family, Bessie got *The Sun News-Pictorial*. Scottie's uncle got *The Age*, but there was less information in that paper than in *The Sun*. The disgruntled former teacher was one Bernard Sumpter, aged 28. *The Sun* (wink, wink) let on he was known as "Bernie". Tumbling over a high wooden fence behind the school, Bernie more or less landed on and was forcibly apprehended by Mr H. Ganz, a citizen who noticed the flicker of flames while taking Karl, his Doberman Pinscher, for a late night walk. Karl, *The Sun News-Pictorial* reported, showed his teeth and did his sustained, low, threatening growl.

Items found in Bernie's black Morris Major were examined by the Arson Squad and deemed "incriminating". The circumstances of Sumpter's dismissal as an English teacher the previous year were not disclosed; however, readers were told Bernie and his wife, another teacher, "had recently separated", and that he lived alone in Essendon, a suburb handy to both the Calder and Hume highways. Apart from the Kyneton fire, police were also investigating the possibility the accused was responsible for a fire at Bacchus Marsh High during the last summer holidays. The newspapers did not disclose whether Sumpter had ever taught in the schools mentioned, but we knew he had never worked at Kyneton. The theory was that his grievance was with the Education Department rather than specific schools, although why he targeted country high schools when he had plenty to choose from right there in Melbourne was never explained. All Sumpter ever said on this was that he liked "a drive in the country".

Don't we all?

III

The third fire was hardly a fire at all. It would normally be seen as no more than arbitrary impishness, but it had consequences and its significance eventually outshone its puny flames. You could say it became the grating hinge upon which this narrative swings.

It happened at the end of the week we went back after term holidays. During the holidays four small prefabs had arrived on Wide Load trucks and were dropped in a row beside the girls' netball court. In the early hours of Friday morning the neighbour on that side of the school was woken by his barking dog. He and his wife managed to get their garden hose onto the fire and pretty well extinguish it before the brigade arrived. All the same, everybody — volunteer firemen, Porkie Veal and Sergeant McPherson — were mightily annoyed at once again being called out in the middle of a cold night. This time, to make things even more interesting, they had to contend with a dense fog.

Who knows just how annoyed the Arson Squad's three wise men were? Despite the patches of lingering mist in the hollows on the way up from the city, they and their dark blue Falcon were on the scene early. But they didn't hang around and we didn't need their eagle eyes to discern this botched job was not the work of whoever did the preceding one. If — and, really, it was a big IF — this pathetic effort was meant to cloud the case against Bernie Sumpter by suggesting that whoever set the first fire was still at large, it didn't work.

When Sumpter appeared in a Melbourne court charged with arson at Broadford and Kyneton, the police said they were confident the recent small fire at Kyneton was a soon to be resolved local matter. Sumpter admitted the Broadford fire (How could he not?) but pleaded not guilty to the charge over Kyneton High's big fire. Bail was granted but the cops let it be known Sumpter was also their main suspect for the Bacchus Marsh fire, which they were investigating with determination. Nothing more was revealed about Bernie's obscure marital troubles but — heigh ho! — *The Sun* ran a photograph of "Bernie the Arsonist".

It was official: Sumpter never taught at Kyneton. Not at Bacchus Marsh or Broadford either. The only country school he ever worked at was Hopetoun, in the Mallee, as a new graduate contractually obliged to go bush for a few years. He had then been at several Melbourne schools and his dispute with the Education Department arose while he was at Essendon. Evidence concerning his "medical history", along with the specific matters leading to the termination of his employment, would be submitted at the proper time and in the proper place.

Meanwhile, after the holidays we found the mess from the destroyed classroom block cleared away and concrete footings in place for a new brick and tile six-classroom building. Construction would be finished by the end of the school year, with furnishings and equipment installed before the start of first term in February. Porkie told us we must box on and do our best in those dog boxes at the edge of the girls' playground.

Concerning which — a few hours' carpentry and

a quick paint job saw the damaged classroom back in service first thing the following Monday.

Did I think Scottie did it? Others certainly did. I mean, you wouldn't put it past him. He was such a ratbag, so impulsive, it could have been a spur of the moment thing in the middle of the night.

Anyway, regardless of whatever I thought I knew, I had to be seen to ask. I did so in a joking manner and Scottie denied it with matching flippancy, but I had to give him the benefit of the doubt and I told all the other kids I believed him. I stuck to him and I sincerely believe that helped his situation. It was the least I could do. And, you know, right through to the end, when he was way past reasons to lie, he always denied starting any but that last, final fire.

Scottie didn't initially think Alan Baker did the small prefab fire. I asked him directly and remember how he shrugged and said Alan would have done a proper job. When we first surveyed the scene, Scottie was genuinely mystified. We talked and decided it could have been anybody. More than likely some pathetic copycat from the lower school, I said. Strangely, it never seemed to occur to Scottie that Alan may have deliberately botched it to throw suspicion elsewhere.

It was after the prefab fire that the one out at Watson's farm back in the autumn was remembered. People returned to the talk about kids playing with matches. Perhaps McPherson had been a little too quick to push the matter off his desk by blaming yobbos up from Melbourne.

As many of you must have discovered from bitter experience, the lightest whiff of suspicion is sometimes the most corrosive. Porkie and the Sergeant got it into their heads that Ronald Scott was not above suspicion. He had come to their attention and he fitted the bill.

It took Porkie five minutes flat that Friday morning to discover Scottie had been demonstrating the properties of flash powder to a not so select audience in the locker room earlier in the week. A few minutes later Stiffy Glover returned to the headmaster's office, one hand firmly gripping Scottie by the elbow and the other gingerly holding a short-fused, big thrupenny bunger. He found it, together with a box of matches (Exhibit B), "concealed" at the back of Scottie's locker. It didn't matter what Scottie said, the headmaster was on the blower to McPherson like a shot, reporting that he had a pupil with pyromaniac tendencies. "I think the lad is not quite right in the head," he said into the phone, staring wide-eyed at the unhinged boy before him.

It was then that Scottie bolted.

He snatched the bunger, side stepped Stiffy and was out the door and through Minnie's office before any of them knew what was happening. Everybody in the building heard the loud echoing of his pounding footfalls as he fled down the long corridor. Kids in the Arts room saw him, firework brandished in his fist, execute a faultless right-angle skidding turn to then hurtle along the east wing gallery. He took the wide concrete steps down past the ladies' staffroom to the assembly yard in a couple of leaping strides and was half way down the terraced slope toward the bike sheds before poor old Stiffy pulled up wheezing at the top of the steps. From there he watched the fugitive race across the sports field clutching what looked like a dull red relay baton. By the time Porkie joined his deputy, Scottie had cleared the ditch at the far end of the field and with a smooth duck and weave was through the strained-wire fence and off school grounds. He didn't look back or slacken his pace as he streaked across the adjoining paddock, up the rise toward Boundary Road.

"He's heading home," Stiffy told Porkie.

"That's a relief," the big man replied, wondering how many Quick-Eze remained in his desk drawer.

Those who saw the headmaster lumber back to his office said they could not remember ever seeing him so grim-faced. "White as a sheet," said Minnie. "Black as thunder," said McPherson, who arrived with one of his constables a few minutes later. After a very brief conversation, the Sergeant drove on to Scottie's place.

It was a surprise to me to learn that monster firecracker was back in Scottie's locker. Mind you, the few minutes we had together first thing that morning had been taken up examining and discussing the latest piece of arson. I heard about the cracker during the boys' locker inspection Porkie called as soon as the cops left in pursuit of Scottie. We were all lined up and assembled in the yard while Stiffy and a couple of other teachers worked their way around the lockers with master keys. If everything was in order, the locker was closed; if not, the offending items were placed at the front for Porkie's inspection and verdict. One kid had half a bottle of fortified plonk but, otherwise, the haul was pretty much as to be expected: cigarettes and matches, shanghais and a few sharp knives. After all his boasting about his stash of dirty magazines Phillip Baron's locker was as clean as a whistle, not even one *Adam* magazine. There was some talk later of a packet of condoms being found in Ken Armstrong's, but Phillip said Ken just made that up to get attention. A piss-poor, feeble thing to say, but he was probably right. Nothing of interest in my locker, thank Christ.

Alan Baker's was clean, too. While everybody else was trying to get a look at what was coming to light, he took himself off to sit on a bench and write stuff in his flipping notebook. I watched him, and he knew I had my eye on him, but he never even looked my way. I almost went over and said something, but then I remembered what Scottie said that day in Melbourne: "He'll keep."

Sergeant McPherson didn't catch up with me until the following morning, the Saturday. He phoned Dad at work last thing Friday and asked him to bring me into the police station for a chat. As was later remarked by my mother, this arrangement spared my parents the neighbourly attentions aroused by a cop car parked outside your house. Despite Mum's wounded silence and loud looks, I didn't realize how serious it all was until Scottie gingerly knocked on our backdoor after tea that evening. Dad went out and quietly but firmly ordered him to get in our car, which he meekly did and was driven home.

At the station the following morning Dad detained the Sergeant in the corridor but I heard enough to know Scottie's visit was being reported. I wasn't sure how damaging that report was to Scottie until we finally had a chance to talk a week later.

Ensconced before their telly, Mr and Mrs Scott had no idea their chastened but ever studious son was out and about the town after dark. Scottie had timed his excursion so as to be back in time to watch The Twilight Zone, but he didn't take into account my father's decisiveness. He thought he would see Dad off by thanking him for the lift, quickly and quietly getting out of the car to sneak down the side driveway ... but, no, Dad had a different idea and the Scotts' front door bell was rung.

Apart from the fact that his room was a sleep-out from which he could come and go pretty much as he pleased, I think what ultimately weighed against Scottie was geography — the map of the town. His way home after doing the runner from Porkie's office was the same seven-minute walk he took to and from school every day.

Other than a quick dash across a foggy Boundary Road, he could have carried stuff to set a fire at the school without anyone seeing a thing.

Coming from the other side of town, Alan Baker had to cover twice the distance. He also had to cross the main street, which in those days was still part of Calder Highway and so had orange neon street lights beading off in either direction in the mist. Alan's problem wouldn't have been just getting to the school, but getting home after the alarm was raised. After all, he lived only a few streets from the fire station. Even in the fog, he had a much riskier route. What's more, Alan's parents were prepared to swear their son could not have left the family abode without their knowledge, an assertion Sergeant McPherson considered substantiated by his personal inspection of the Bakers' house and back garden.

The subject of Geography would get a better airing later in the week. When the Sergeant interviewed me that Saturday morning, he was more interested in History, Chemistry and, for want of a better word, Psychology. He wanted to know what Scottie and I got up to in Melbourne; what we bought and where. "Did his parents know he was trying to buy a damned snake!?" He wanted to know what we discussed about the school fire and — "I'm just trying to understand this!" — Why did I reckon Ronald made such accusations about young Baker? Why did Mr Veal think I deserved a dose of the cuts along with my silly mate? How seriously did I take all that occult nonsense that so fascinated Master Scott?

Not wishing to exhaust my limited quota of "Don't know" shrugs, I did my best to truthfully answer the questions. Perhaps it was because my father was present and fidgeting, but the interview never became an interrogation. Notes were taken, and I don't know what use was ever made of them, but I was not asked to sign anything. We were just having a chat. Which, when you understand how these things work in country towns, was fairly serious.

Mostly, the Sergeant wanted to know about that thrupenny bunger Scottie *said* he found in his locker. There was newspaper talk of banning them and, anyhow, they were not readily available in our town, even in the week before Bonfire Night when fireworks were sold legally. So where did it come from?

With Dad sitting behind me I had to admit Scottie and I bought a few under the counter from Wilson's newsagency last November. Dad confirmed we let them off at our place on Guy Fawkes Night. All or some of them was a moot point. Actually, Bonfire Night at our place was a bit of a tricky subject for Dad because he was in the habit of using the general commotion to test fire three or four of the muzzleloaders in his gun collection. McPherson must have known about it — the rest of the town did — but, like I said, he and Dad marched together. Anyway, the key question was whether I had seen a thrupenny bunger in Scottie's possession in recent months. To which I could truthfully answer that the only one I'd seen him with was the one he pulled out of his locker just before the holidays.

"And ... ever see anybody else with one?"

I shook my head. Not me. I'd seen nothing.

The Sergeant nodded agreeably, looked out the window and apparently contemplated what the weather might do for the rest of the day. "What," he asked as he quietly turned his gaze back to me, "makes you think young Baker put that cracker in your mate's locker?"

"Because ... well, because he was getting even. Because we had, you know, searched his locker and Scottie had been saying Alan had something to do with burning down the classroom block."

89

"Yes, he did, didn't he? But leaving aside possible motives, how do you know the firework in question was Alan Baker's? What proof?"

"He had some. They reckon he souped them up and put one down the Sullivans' chimney. He must've bought them from Ma Wilson's."

"She doesn't remember that."

Oh.

"But," the Sergeant went on, "if he did, he won't get any more there this year." He gave a dry little laugh as he said, "*Mrs* Wilson will not be stocking that particular item in future. You have my permission to spread the word on that score."

I was nodding understanding and agreement when the bunger Scottie made off with the day before suddenly appeared on the Sergeant's desk.

"Assuming this really is the same item Ronald found in his locker a few weeks ago — why didn't he report it?"

"He didn't think Mr Veal would believe him," I replied, calm as a cucumber.

"Really?"

"He thought it'd just get him into more trouble."

"Well, one way or the other, he was right about that, wasn't he? You said Alan Baker souped up crackers. How do you mean? Is that something you and Ronald tried?"

That threw me. I had to confess I didn't really know what Alan had done, it was all hearsay, but before I knew it I admitted Scottie and me had "once or twice" tried to enhance penny bungers. I was quick to add we always ended up with fizzers and had quickly given the idea away as a waste of good fireworks.

Lightly tapping the big firecracker with his indelible pencil, the Sergeant asked if I thought it had been "enhanced". I leaned forward, peered at the area surrounding the short wick and told him I didn't think so. He pressed me to explain what I was looking for and to tell him what we had done in our efforts to strengthen the power of bungers.

I couldn't say whether it was Scottie's or my own innovation, but it was one of those clear cut theories that turn out to be more complicated in practice. From three regular crackers we figured we should get two souped up ones. Using a razor blade or a very sharp, thin knife, you need to open up one for the powder. Then, with the tip of the knife, cut a deep circle in the top of the other crackers and work out the fuse together with a collar of the densely packed paper around it. You have to get that narrow plug out to expose the top of the column of powder through the body of the cracker. You have to go through the top rather than the bottom because the bottom is too thick. Cutting around and removing the fuse has to be very cleanly and evenly done, you must not damage or create a weakness in the barrel of the cracker. We used a razor blade and a nice little pen knife, but we probably should have got hold of a proper scalpel. The second stage of the operation is to tap out as much of the powder from the de-fused crackers and carefully insert something like a large nail or the shaft of a small screwdriver down into the cavity. Work the nail around to slightly widen the cavity and then pour in as much powder as is needed to refill the enlarged space, all the while tapping it firmly down — "It's a bit like loading a muzzleloader," I offered, and then seeing the look McPherson shot at Dad, wished I'd thought of some other analogy. The last thing is to get the fuse back in and reseal the top, but somehow we could never get that bit right. The fuse would burn down and either go out or the top of the cracker would blow out and it would burn out like a Roman candle. A fizzer.

I got a bit carried away and rushed through my

exposition to come to a teetering halt and an awkward silence. McPherson cleared his throat, tapped a Lucky Strike from its pack and lit it. Dropping the dead match in his big brass ashtray, he asked, "What'd you use to seal the tops?"

"Tarzan's Grip!" I fairly blurted, wishing to convey my incredulity that that legendary glue had failed us.

With his cigarette contentedly smouldering away between his index and middle fingers, McPherson picked up the bunger and, eyes half closed, examined both ends. More or less to himself, he said, "I would have thought ..."

I waited to hear what it was that he thought. I was interested. But — bloody hell! — he just held my attention with a wink as he put the cracker back in his desk.

"I hope you two have the sense to never try extracting powder from shotgun cartridges."

I gave an awkward laugh. Dad sat very still. "No, Sir," I lied.

"Hmm. There was a kid up at Castlemaine a few months back had a close shave. Very close shave. Took off his eyebrows. Burnt his hands and face. Very red-faced young fellow looking pretty damned stupid for all the world to see. You and young Scott seem to have quite an interest in chemistry and explosives."

"Science is Scottie's favourite subject," I offered.

"And what about you?"

"I like history."

"Do ya now? Battle of Trafalgar?"

"1805."

"Bannockburn?"

"1314."

"Commanders?"

"Robert the Bruce and Edward II."

The Sergeant leaned back and unlocked a small cupboard behind his desk. What looked like a candle wrapped in wax paper slid across his desk. "Ever seen any of this stuff?"

I had. "My uncle Laurie uses it to blow up stumps."

"The brother-in-law," Dad put in. "He's on a soldier settlement block in the Wimmera."

"What about detonators? Apart from your uncle's place, ever seen them?"

"No, Sir," I answered with enough fright in my voice to sound truthful.

The Sergeant regarded me a moment before nodding at the gelly, "You ever see any of this or a detonator you tell me. Straight away, you tell me. Understand?"

"Yes, Sir."

"Took this off a clown out Redesdale way a few weeks ago," the Sergeant said to Dad. "You might know him. I reckon he thought he was Gelignite Jack," he half laughed with open contempt. "I'll have to hand it in after the court appearance. As for your mate's piece of work," he sighed, and looked at me. "I don't know what can be done with that just yet. Too many people involved ... We'll see."

He then slowly read over his notes. Without looking up and with that casual Inspector Maigret after-thought manner all coppers aspire to, he asked, "Who told you Alan Baker put one down the Sullivan's chimney?"

I daresay I must have looked surprised that he, of all people, would ask that question. "But ... I mean, everybody knew about it."

"What people think and what actually happens are often different things. Did anyone you know ever hear it directly from Alan?"

I shrugged. "Not me. He never talks to us. Maybe some of them older kids in his year ... I never heard anyone say he said he didn't do it."

"Tell me this," the Sergeant leaned forward, all attention, "did anyone other than you or young Scott say they thought Alan Baker had anything to do with burning down the lower school classrooms?"

I had to admit I'd not heard of anyone else suggesting he had.

"No," McPherson confirmed, his voice abruptly official, "it was just you two. See, there you are ... a couple of bunnies caught in the spotlight. You were the ones who started that nonsense. Mr Veal tells me Baker does not have classes in that building and, given that he had no reason to be there, you'd think someone would notice and recall if he had. Whereas," he did the pause-for-effect, "you and Scott have a Geography class there twice a week. Now I'm not accusing you — because, as I'm sure you've heard, we believe we have the culprit in Melbourne — but I want to bring home to you how stupid it is to run around making groundless accusations. As far as I can work out, you just don't like the fellow. That's a bit gutless, don't you think?"

"Yes, Sir," I mumble.

I stare at my hands, study the very interesting frieze of elephants (trunks holding tails) pressed into the ashtray's wide rim; examine my hands again before taking a quick look at the Sergeant's watching eyes. "Yes, Sir," I say again, clearly, to his right shoulder.

Another long and awkward moment.

"All right then, You need to be careful about being led astray by someone with too vivid an imagination. Do your mate a favour! Next time he gets one of his silly ideas, talk him out of it and save us all a lot of buggerizing about! Your parents are upset and worried. And they're not too happy in the Baker household either! As for Mrs Scott ..." The Sergeant trailed off to address my father over my head, "I reckon she's on the verge of a nervous breakdown."

"Umm, that's no good," Dad murmured.

"Mind you ..." McPherson raised his eyebrows and lowered his voice, "nervous woman by nature, if you know what I mean."

Another vague noise from Dad affirmed he did know what the policeman meant.

The Sergeant took a drag of his cigarette and gave his desk a light knuckle rap. "Anyway," his eyes snapped back to me, "you talk sense into your mate. If you can't, and this sort of bullshit comes around again, there will be consequences. Proceedings may be commenced. You understand?"

"Yes, Sir." I nodded with enough energy to leave no doubt I got the message.

"All right, then." The Sergeant clamped his fag in the corner of his mouth, narrowed his eyes against the smoke and started tidying his papers. "I reckon that oughta do it," he said to my father.

"Yeah," Dad drawled, rising, "an' I reckon someone knows he'll get a solid clip behind the lughole if there's any more trouble."

The Sergeant allowed the glimmer of a wan smile as he plucked the cigarette from his mouth and stood to offer his hand to me. He then shook Dad's hand.

One evening a couple of days later Dad chased my brothers off and detained me at the dinner table. He asked whether I remembered seeing Scottie at the football the day Watson's shed went up in smoke. Before I grasped what my answer might imply, I admitted I did not. After he dried the dishes with particular care Dad went up the passage to the phone table and made a call. I tried to overhear but Mum shooed me off and I guessed the call was to McPherson. You didn't have to be Sherlock Holmes to work out this was not going well for Scottie. Not good at all.

I suppose I should have said a few words about Scottie's parents before this. But, let's face it, at that age — fifteen going on sixteen — you're only really interested in those your own age. And, to be honest, Scottie didn't talk about his parents all that much. He did, but he didn't, if you know what I mean.

To me, the single most interesting thing about Mr Jefferson Scott was that he was a slaughterman. He wasn't a burly bloke, and with his wire-framed glasses and neat casual jacket he looked more like a mild-mannered tally clerk than a slaughterman. But a skilled killer of beasts he was and a strong union man while he was about it. Workday mornings, much of the year before sun-up, he left home with a cut lunch, warmed up his baby blue Morris 1000 van and drove the mile and a bit out of town to the local meatworks. There he changed into his work gear, cut the throats of sheep and stuck pigs all the live long day, showered, changed back into his civvies, combed his hair and drove home. He usually arrived back mid-afternoon, just before Scottie came home from school, but because his father immediately took an hour's nap, Scottie rarely saw him before the evening meal.

I didn't have a lot to do with Mr Scott. He was what you'd call a private person. On the weekends he'd say "G'day, young fella," and disappear into the lounge room with a book or a magazine. I never saw his skinning and boning knives, even though Scottie told me they were regularly brought home for sharpening. When I once asked Scottie which footy team his Old Man barracked for, he told me his father came from some place near Sydney and so wasn't that interested in Australian Rules football. In fact, and I remember how Scottie said this with clear approval, he told me his father had been known to mockingly refer to the game as "aerial ping-pong". When I asked about his father's family in New

South Wales, Scottie just shrugged, said his grandparents died when his father was young, and changed the subject.

Somewhere along the way I heard Scottie had a twin brother who died at birth. I believe this had something to do with why Mrs Scott could not have any more children. We never discussed it.

Mrs Scott's name was Irene. One day Scottie showed me an old EP 45 disc from a pile of records his parents had from way back. It was a Decca release of The Weavers and one of its tracks was "Goodnight Irene". Scottie got a bit goofy about it, which I didn't think was very cool, but maybe he knew something more than he said about the occasions his father played it. I dunno, it was all a bit "So what?"

I was more interested in another track on the record: "On Top of Old Smokey". My cousin Don from Korumburra taught me a version of that song. Those farm boys with older brothers who'd done National Service knew all the dirty songs and jokes. The first verse of Don's rendition went:

On top of old smokey,
all covered with snow
I saw Roy Rogers
root Marilyn Monroe.

Scottie laughed but he put the record away and never mentioned it again.

Mrs Scott did some casual, make-ends-meet dressmaking at home. Alterations, mostly, but every so often she was commissioned to do a bridesmaid's dress or a ball gown. She also made some of her own frocks and skirts, decent yet pert apparel that quietly accentuated her own trim figure. Later on I overheard Mum opine that Mrs Scott's "party frocks" had "a bit of flair". Or was it "a bit of flounce"? That was probably true enough, but the cardigans and pullovers she knitted every other year for Mr Scott and Ronald were sturdy but fairly standard stuff. I don't want to boast, but my mother's multi-coloured Fair Isle jumpers won prizes.

I liked Mrs Scott — she made first-rate toasted cheese sandwiches — but her bright and cheerful manner was always a little too intense, too busy. She laughed too loud, a little more readily than other mums, and you were never quite sure why she found what she found amusing to be *so* amusing. I don't think for one moment she did it on purpose, but something in that mix of sudden raucousness and half closed, watching eyes made it hard for a growing boy to feel entirely relaxed.

I understood, instantly, what the Sergeant meant by calling Mrs Scott a "nervous woman". She was jittery, no other word for it. She talked fast and sculpted the air as she did so. She smoked a lot and used a cigarette holder; maybe not quite as long as Auntie Mame's, but in that league. Nobody was so unkind as to refer to it as "an affectation", but they surely thought so. After the Scotts left Kyneton some of Mum's acquaintances settled upon labelling Irene Scott an "artistic type of woman". I suppose they thought that was being charitable. Perhaps it was.

Remember, Scottie was an only child in the days when most families had three or four kids — and that was before you started counting the Catholics. In my family (we were C of E), for instance, I had three younger brothers. Then, beyond that, I had dozens of cousins. Scottie didn't even have one. The only relative I knew of was that childless aunt, his mother's sister, out in the smug eastern suburbs of Melbourne.

While it was true Scottie's parents could calmly discuss important matters and generally keep a closer eye on him than parents in the hurly-burly of managing a swarm of squabbling kids, it was also the case that he had greater independence than other kids. He grew up with the privacy and responsibility of his own room, something the rest of us could only daydream about.

Whatever freedom Ronnie enjoyed in normal circumstances, the developing situation saw the Scotts' kitchen table hosting some serious, no nonsense discussions. He promised he would keep out of trouble. Promised.

His parents believed him and gave him their trust. But really, ask yourself, how many modern parents grasp the difference between trusting sincere intentions as opposed to grappling with a child's true nature?

As for everybody else ... Heaven knows, small towns the world over have tolerated and cared for their own wild boys and village idiots from time out of mind. All the same, there are limits. When inherent silliness combines with a reckless propensity to play with matches, to mess around with explosives and flammable materials — then best keep a careful eye on the lad in question.

Scottie was watched by his parents, Sergeant McPherson, Porkie Veal, Stiffy Glover and the other teachers, kids at school, the nosy neighbours — everybody. Being the talk of the town, it didn't take long for opinions to be exchanged and for judgements to be made. I sensed the reflected chill when Scottie and I went up the street Saturday morning. Ma Wilson had reason enough to be miffed, having recently put up with a semi-official visit from himself of the polished buttons and big boots, clumping about and making a show of taking notes. But other adults also acted differently, either by being noticeably reserved or so volubly jocose as to make anybody uneasy.

The fact that Scottie's only proven or admitted offence was searching another kid's locker was lost behind the accepted verdict that he had tried to burn down the replacement prefabs and blame the dirty deed on that very same kid he had already wronged — to wit, the bank manager's son. Then, too, the story of Scottie snatching the big bunger off Porkie's desk and doing a runner reminded people of when he defied old Hogan and pulled that stunt of dancing around on the roof of the primary school. The boy had a history. He was odd. It was a shame to have to say it, they all said, but one could be forgiven for thinking his airy-fairy mother must have dropped him on his head when he was a baby.

But listen, really, in looking over what I have written I see plodding clues dropped and nodding hints winked: "after the Scotts left Kyneton", and so forth. Although I understand busy, modern readers (eager souls brought up on cut-to-the-chase headlines) may be enticed to sneak a peek at the final pages to see "what happened", I wouldn't want you, treasured and sensitive reader, to feel manipulated by these all too common and somewhat transparent devices of narrative suspense. I, too, am inherently uneasy about such authorial games of Cluedo, and concerned that such doings risk the appearance of disrespecting the memory of what happened to Scottie.

See, there, I've gone and done it again ... "what happened to Scottie".

All right, so here goes, let's get to the hard facts of what happened to Scottie.

A few weeks short of his sixteenth birthday Ronald Scott accidentally set himself alight and suffered third-degree burns to his arms, upper torso and face. He was hideously scarred for life. The last time I saw him, more than a year after the accident, I could barely recognize him. Scottie had years of skin grafts, suffered terribly and finally shot himself when he was in his mid-twenties.

His mother was zombied-out on medications — the poor woman's hair turned white — and Mr Scott had to give up work to look after her.

Now you want to know how it came to pass that my friend, after all the strife he'd been in and the clear warnings he'd been given, was still fooling about with gunpowder, petrol and matches.

I can only tell you what I saw and heard. Or, rather, what I now remember of what I saw and heard all those years ago. I know I must steer clear of what the philosophers term a teleological argument (crudely: cart before the horse); nevertheless, in telling you what I know I cannot do so other than through the prism of half a century of hindsight and regret.

One pitfall I know we must avoid is that of leaning too heavily on a psychoanalytical reading of events. It was the reaching for psychological explanations (all the rage in Yankee films and TV shows at the time) that led to the speculative whispers about Scottie's accident maybe not being an accident. People assumed the lad was at the end of his tether, they got wind of his interest in Eastern mysticism, they had seen that terrible image of a Buddhist's self-immolation in Saigon the year before, they put two and two together and ... well, I'm telling you, that's all bullshit!

There was no motive, conscious or otherwise. It was an accident. That has to be stated in no uncertain terms. The kindest thing I can say about those Clever Dicks who said the opposite is that they simply did not know what they were talking about.

I'm sorry, but the accusation — the unwarranted accusation — that Scottie deliberately did that to himself is something that continues to upset me. It was a wicked thing to say.

Anyway, putting aside that raw wound ...

I freely admit to not understanding the finer points of the theory and practice of psychology, but I do believe it has very limited application in Scottie's story. What happened to him may very well have been due, in some *small* part, to his character, but the circumstances he had to deal with were created by those around him and I reckon the dynamics of that situation are more usefully described — although not entirely explained — by the terminology and within the framework of anthropology, sociology, astrology or some other university taught social science.

I do not say Scottie had cultivated his notoriety after the school fires, but he did secretly relish it and thought it gave him some status. And it did do that, I think, but mostly on the mistaken belief he had attempted to light that second fire at the school and sort of got away with it. I knew he had done no such thing. But that was sort of beside the point because, make no mistake about this, the thing about a small town's verdict is that once reached, it is not easily changed.

IV

The fourth fire was when Bonfire Night went off a night too early, and without the customary bang. A person or persons unknown put a match to the giant pyre the Lions Club had built on the showground oval. An erect telegraph pole festooned with old tyres, piled around with logs, plywood packing cases and several truckloads of combustible rubbish, it was topped by a scarecrow Guy Fawkes. A final cladding of recently lopped, resin oozing cypress pine boughs gave the forty-foot work something of a Christmas tree look.

All concerned were rightly pleased with their efforts. Doc Connell, suitably jollified and sporting his new Bolex 16mm movie camera, filmed the stages of construction and was geared up to record for posterity what was promoted as the biggest communal bonfire in the town's history. There had been drizzle on Monday, but that general dampening of the surrounds suited Tom Wedge and his men, who would attend the event in their official capacities.

On Tuesday, Melbourne Cup Day (Polo Prince at twelve to one), the Fire Chief announced that, barring strong winds blowing sparks all over the place, he saw no reason why Thursday night's occasion should not go ahead as planned. Confident anticipation suffused the town.

On Wednesday the Kyneton Cup (Fairwood at short odds) was run without major incident on or off the field. The first race started at noon and the last event's trophies were being handed out by five o'clock. By then horse floats were slowing traffic on all roads out of town and the bookies were settling up among themselves in a private tent, closely watched by the extra police brought in from Bendigo and Melbourne.

It had been a big day for Sergeant McPherson, a busy day, but he managed to front the back bar of the Royal in time for a last drink with his small group of confidants. The Sergeant let it be known that he had been told on the QT there had been a plunge on Fairwood. Constable O'Reilly's comment that bookies were always the ultimate winners was ruefully agreed to.

All seemed well. It had been a long day. A good meal and a quiet evening at home murmured their blandishments. But then, as they walked away from the pub, a niggling "What if?" prompted the Sergeant to ask the Constable to meet him back at the Police Station after they had eaten.

The pair arrived at the showgrounds about eight o'clock and advertised their presence by conducting a flashlight search. With the moon setting early and low clouds pushing across the range from the south, it was pretty damned dark. Even so, when they sat halfway up in the grandstand and let their eyes adjust to the background glow of street lights from the Housing Commission estate, it was possible to discern any movement in the open space around that imposing solid black cone on the oval. Rugged up in his old army greatcoat and equipped with a Thermos of black tea, McPherson let the recently-married O'Reilly off for the night, asking him to drive the police car back to the station and park it where it could be seen from the street. The Sergeant stayed, listening to the night. Not allowing himself even one cigarette, he sat there three hours, thinking and remembering, as one does;

he sat there until the dozen or so patrons of old Talkie's Wednesday night Horror flick had time to get home and lock their doors, until a cold, drizzling rain set in from the south. Finally, feeling his age, he stood and stretched, lit a well earned smoke, made another show of torchlight about the place and, savouring the policeman's ancient role of night watchman, walked home through the sleeping town. By midnight, when most of the street lights went off, the Sergeant had sunk into his wife-warmed bed and settled on the floor of sleep's ocean.

Then, just before one o'clock: disaster, calamity, debacle. The town was roused by the fire siren's dire clangour. McPherson's wife later told Mary O'Reilly he had sworn "like a trooper".

Ordering his wife to phone the constables, McPherson drove like a madman back to the showgrounds to see the bonfire in full blaze, roaring in the rain. Those who turned out to witness the spectacle also heard the Sergeant uttering a wide range of profanities and obscenities. But then, as soon as he saw the brigade had things under control, he disappeared. O'Reilly and the other bloke (I forget his name) knew where he went, but they weren't telling, being busy sorting out who had seen what.

Sergeant McPherson drove around past the Housing estate and along Boundary Road to pull up outside the Scott's, slamming his car door to announce his arrival. His torch flashing in all directions, he stomped up the front path. As he mounted the front step intent upon thumping on the front door, he noticed a light on inside the house. Indeed, Scottie's father snapped on the porch light and opened the door as the copper raised his fist to deliver the first knock.

The slaughterman and the policeman stared at each other through the fly-screen door.

McPherson didn't miss a beat. "You understand," he

said politely but firmly, "I'm here to make sure your son is at home and has not been out tonight."

At that moment, in pyjamas and a dressing gown to match that of his father's (Mrs Scott's work), Scottie appeared beside his father. "I'm here and I have not been out," he said quietly but clearly.

Mr Scott cleared his throat to speak, but was momentarily distracted by his wife entering their bedroom and closing the door behind her.

"I trust you have no objection to my having a quick look at Ronald's room and his bike," McPherson went on, lowering his voice.

"We heard the siren," Scottie's father nodded over the Sergeant's shoulder at the glow of the fire, "and came out to have a look. I woke Ronald. He's been here all night."

"Well, I'm pleased to hear that. I am. I'll get a statement from you later, but you understand that right now I need to have a look for myself ... so ... I can make my report."

Scottie told me his father and McPherson stared hard at each other for an unnervingly long time before he released the catch and invited the policeman into the house. With Scottie bringing up the rear, his father led McPherson through the house to the sleep-out. The rumpled bed got a cursory glance, but Scottie's shoes and the clothes inside the wardrobe were examined with some attention. Shown Scottie's bike, dry and inside the locked garage, McPherson ruffled Scottie's dry hair and gave a dry laugh. He offered Mr Scott his hand and by way of apology said, "This is a bad business."

The Sergeant was back at the showgrounds at first light. His men had knocked pickets into the ground and run a cordon rope around the crime scene — there was always at least one bloody clown who thought he could and should conduct his own forensic examination. A quick look through that morning's country edition of

The Sun didn't find any mention of the Kyneton fire, although it was probably in the later city editions. Someone said it had been mentioned on the wireless, near the end of the ABC's morning news. Having served in New Guinea, Doug McPherson had no time for Yanks, but that morning he was pleased the news was all about Lyndon Baines Johnson comprehensively seeing off Mr Goldwater to be re-elected (or, strictly speaking, elected in his own right) President of those United States.

Doc Connell took upon himself the sobering duty of filming grim-faced men in overcoats standing around in the grey dawn, mutely regarding the smouldering heap. He offered the film to McPherson, should he or the Arson Squad require it for evidence.

The Arson Squad!? Well, now ... Ha ha! Where oh where are those dapper gents with their Ronson lighters when you need them? Ha ha! It seemed the Sergeant would have to conduct the investigation, take the official photographs and write the report himself. But — Ha! — "Yeah, thanks Doc, I'll let you know ... just keep it to yourself for the time being."

After Doc had been given the time of day and the bloke from the local paper granted a short statement, after the numerous outraged Lions and various sticky-beaks had seen enough and gone to work, after the last kids were chased off to school, McPherson and his two men set about raking through the mess. They didn't know what they were looking for but they recognised it as soon as Joe O'Reilly turned it over.

A medium sized, classic style alarm clock with a hammer between two bells on top.

And there, next to it, some blackened glass, perhaps from test tubes or beakers.

Ah ha!

The Sergeant asked his officers to step back, took a

couple of photos and, with the injunction that nothing was to be further disturbed, immediately drove to his office to phone Melbourne.

The Arson Squad and their slightly bespattered station wagon were there just after lunch; accompanied by a Channel 7 news crew. We later heard the cops, TV van hard on their tail, were seen coming up the Calder Highway, clocking at least 75 miles an hour. Believe you me, your genuine, fair-dinkum incendiary device always rearranges priorities.

The town was pleased to have its one minute and twenty seconds on the Melbourne telly that night. Straight after the first ad break a fresh-faced young man with a wind-baffled microphone almost as big as his head explained everything while, in the background, Sergeant McPherson could be clearly seen pointing out this and that to his attentive colleagues from the Arson Squad. To McPherson's surprise, a ten-second clip of Doc Connell's film (rush developed courtesy of Channel 7) showing the bonfire being built was also included in the report. A few Lions, claiming to recognise themselves (but nobody else) in the shaky hand-held panning shot, opined that the Doc ought to invest in a tripod.

Such chatter and amusement was hardly a silver lining to what was a very dark cloud. Although a few small fires were quickly thrown together in backyards and on spare blocks, it was generally agreed that year's Bonfire Night was a flop. The adults felt obliged to put on a show for the kids, so fireworks already bought were dutifully let off. The crackle of a string of Tom Thumbs here and the pop of a bunger there were occasionally enlivened by the sparking whizz of a Catherine wheel or the whoosh and flowering stars of a rocket, but it all fizzled out early. There were no reports of burns or other injuries, no satisfying thumps from muskets discharged in our backyard. Scottie stayed home.

People were stung, pissed off. The Lions, all volunteers, had gone to a lot of trouble and expense. The monies expected to be raised from their venture's modest entrance fee would have gone towards the building of a new and much-needed old people's home.

Within the anger, however, there was also the grit of fear. The deliberate destruction of the bonfire was universally understood as an act of sheer, pointless bastardry; something truly spiteful. Not only was there a *pyromaniac* loose in our midst, this one was smart and brazen. As with the initial reaction to the first school fire, before it was slated to Bernie Sumpter (who, as some shrewdly noted, continued to deny responsibility), there was the disquieting likelihood the malevolent presence behind the bonfire event would turn out to be someone we knew; a gloating lunatic, sneakily thumbing his nose at us.

Close by the alarm clock and glass vials, the police found four big torch batteries, copper wires and an old paint tin. The makings were all there, except the ignition agent and the accelerant — probably kero or metho — which, naturally, had been consumed. It was a cunning piece of work that could have been assembled in a cardboard box, carried to the crime scene in an ordinary duffle bag and shoved deep into the layers of pine branches. Almost certainly set running in the early hours of the night before, it must have been ticking away while McPherson watched so diligently from the grandstand. He wondered, had he stood near enough and listened, would he have heard it?

The ignition agent? Probably something any kid with a chemistry set could get his hands on. Magnesium powder, potassium nitrate ...

Flash powder!

After discussions with his colleagues and a quick call to Melbourne, Detective-Sergeant Whelan of the Arson Squad stayed overnight (Guy Fawkes Night), comfortable and well-fed at the Royal. The plan was for him and McPherson to attend the Scott residence first thing the following morning. They turned up before Scottie left for school and Mr Scott, fetched from his workplace by Constable O'Reilly, arrived back a few minutes later in his own blue van. The father was served the search warrant, but the son was the suspect.

By all accounts the business was conducted with formal courtesy. Although there was a cursory inspection of the kitchen and washhouse, the areas of interest were Scottie's sleep-out (informally searched only 30 hours before), the garage and the adjoining toolshed with its large and well-equipped work bench. Drawers, boxes and tins were opened and examined; cluttered dark corners under the bench were searched, with particular attention paid to areas of broken cobwebs. For about an hour questions were officially asked and civil answers recorded. Scottie was asked to sign a declaration that the flash powder he purchased the previous winter was gone, as was the fuse paper, and that neither item had been replaced. Mr Scott counter-signed, verifying his son's statement was given without coercion. He also signed his own statement that no such materials had been in his house since the previous trouble. In fact, Ronald had not been permitted any fireworks at all — his Bonfire Night had been to sit on the front steps and watch the occasional striggling rocket arc up the sky.

For form's sake Whelan scraped a few dusty samples into small plastic jars, but it was plain to see that nothing incriminating had been discovered. Noticing a set of American whetstones, Whelan tried to start a conversation about the relative merits of natural and artificial sharpening stones, but the flint-eyed slaughterman merely replied that it depended on what was being sharpened.

At the end of proceedings, as the police were about to leave, Mr Scott looked Sergeant McPherson in the face and quietly told him, "You're looking in the wrong place."

McPherson drew himself up and shot back, a little too loudly, a little too aggressively, "Is that so? And where do you think is the *right* place?"

Mr Scott did not flinch. He didn't blink and he didn't step back. "I don't know," he answered, with a glance to ensure Whelan was paying attention, "but I think it's about time you made inquiries elsewhere."

McPherson compressed his lips, considering his reply, but Mr Scott cut him off: "I've gotta get back to work. The line's been slowed ... there's unwatered stock in the killing pens."

"You're free to go about your business. Thank you for your assistance."

Without asking whether his son was also free to go, Mr Scott told him to take his school bag and get in the Morris.

"We can drop him off, it's on our way back," McPherson offered, conciliation personified. "Save you the time."

Glancing at his fretting wife, Mr Scott's voice was level as he said it would be better if he were the one to explain to Mr Veal the cause of Ronald's lateness.

Only Minnie Mouse witnessed what passed between Messrs Veal and Scott. She correctly refused to repeat it word-for-word, but nevertheless let a few interested parties know Mr Scott made it clear he would not tolerate any suggestion his son was in any way associated with the recent fires; and would formally complain to the Minister for Education should anyone at the school be so foolish as to say Ronald was "not quite right in the head".

Minnie had a brief waltz with her conscience but could

not resist the thrill of repeating Mr Scott's parting shot at Porkie: "Now, if you will excuse me, I have animals to kill."

Needless to say, half the town heard that timeless remark repeated over that night's dinner table. The other half ... well, they'd already heard it before they sat down to their meal.

The force of an accusation is not diminished because it is murmured. The blunt instrument can be as deadly as the sharp. Poor Scottie was damned whichever way he jumped. Silence was almost an admission of guilt and even mild denial looked like protesting too much.

These days there are names and medications for whatever afflicted Scottie. Back then, he was just an easily led flibbertigibbet. I think he more or less understood his best bet was to stand still, to keep his mouth shut, to not blink and let the storm pass — but, as eager as the sorcerer's apprentice, when temptation came along he just couldn't help himself. Of course, as most of us know from experience, holding ourselves aloof is easier said than done. I mean, truthfully, how do you think you would cope with the sting of a false accusation? Especially one whispered behind hands rather than plainly stated?

The way it worked was mothers told their kids to keep away from Scottie. Some contact was unavoidable, but otherwise he was *verboten*. Kids were told not to talk to or be seen with him. Above all, they were never to be seen *alone* with him.

Actually, quite a few kids, usually in small groups in the clammy privacy of the locker room, contrived to hear Scottie's side of the matter. I don't know how many believed his denials, but some seemed prepared to withhold judgement, even though they were obliged to heed their parents' orders. There were others who jibed him with the inevitable "Gawn! You can tell us!" One bloke just assumed Scottie did it and went for the jugular by asking how to build a bomb, all the while repeating to Scottie (and me) that the bonfire job was "shit-hot, brilliant". I say "and me" because that particular prick, who went on to pursue his own amateurish criminal career, made no bones of the fact that he saw me as an accessory, Scottie's partner-in-crime.

Other than suggesting I start studying for the exams, my parents did not restrict my contact or ask me to break with my friend. Looking back, I believe it probably would have been easier for me if they had. Sergeant McPherson's injunction that I "talk some sense into my silly mate" shifted and firmed into a directive that I should talk to Scottie with an eye toward getting him to admit his guilt. I was not-so-gently led to stand before and contemplate the stark alternative of being an accomplice or an informer.

The next time we were alone, Scottie and I had a brief, clumsy conversation about this situation. I assured him I'd never dob a mate and I remember his fixed grin as he assured me there was nothing to tell anyway. He never hid his interest in chemistry, fireworks and all that shit, and he admitted to all sorts of other stuff that could have got him into trouble — but he steadfastly denied starting any fires. When the inevitable conversation with my father came around, I honestly reported that I believed Scottie's protestations of innocence.

Although Scottie didn't want anyone to know he still thought Alan Baker responsible for the big school fire, I must own up that I did pass that contention on to Dad. I told him Scottie said: "He's watching me and I'm watching him, but he'll make a mistake." Dad frowned and rubbed his mouth in a worried kind of way. He said nothing more to me, but I'm sure Scottie's remark found a certain ear in the back bar of the Royal.

Even the hullabaloo of Phillip Baron being suspended didn't distract the town's beady eye from Scottie.

Phillip was caught flogging his pood one lunchtime in the girls' bike shed. Fumbling himself back into his unbuttoned fly, he was dragged out by the ear by Miss Andersen. The girl's phys ed teacher was a well-built young woman and more than a match for the white-faced masturbator. The indignant Amazon loudly let everybody know there was a filthy, filthy animal in their midst. (We knew! We knew!) A brace of male teachers came to her assistance, took charge of Phillip and marched him off to Porkie's office. Miss Andersen, a red-head, paused a moment in the sudden silence to wipe her hands on her tunic and gather her breath. Those who saw the frolicsome scene all swore she then looked around at the hundred or so agog children staring at her — and blushed the deepest crimson imaginable. It was an amusing distraction, but the collective gaze soon drifted back to dwell on Scottie.

And me.

I want to be clear: Alan Baker approached me. It was about midday on a Saturday in the middle of November and I was loitering on the Post Office steps observing the effects of skittish breezes on cigarette butts and other small rubbish in the gutter. I remember there was one of those lolly wrappers with film stars' biographies on them. I picked it up and read that Marilyn Monroe was born in Los Angeles in 1926. Died there, too. But the slip of waxed paper about to go down the drain in Kyneton didn't say anything about that.

Alan came up from Mrs Macklin's cake and pie shop, a few doors down the street toward the picture theatre. He had a big, fat, piping fresh sausage roll sticking out of a greasy brown paper bag. The whole thing was dripping tomato sauce and it smelt very damn good.

He stood next to me, blowing on the hot meat and pastry and noisily sucking in his breath as he nipped off manageable bites. He was older and taller than me and stood that wee bit too close for comfort. I was about to walk away when he asked, polite as poison, if we could have a word.

I stared at him but, other than a swift scan up and down the street, he just continued with the task at dealing with his sausage roll. He wasn't exactly friendly, but he wasn't giving off his usual hostile aura. Then, apparently suddenly remembering his manners, he swallowed, looked at me with his strange eyes and said, "Sorry. If I'd known I was going to bump into you, I'd have got another one. The old duck makes decent sausage rolls, don't she?"

The truth is the truth. I grunted agreement.

"Look, here! We'll have a talk, so why don't we pop back and let me shout you?"

I was torn. But ... I'm the kind of bloke who knows an opening when he sees one.

"Fair dinkum," he said, "I'm flush." Knowing I'd follow, he started back to the pie shop. We didn't talk as he scoffed the remains of his roll, wiped his hands on the emptied bag and dropped it in the bin outside the shop.

The carnal aroma inside the warm shop was bliss. Being lunchtime, Mrs Macklin and Sharon were flat out dispensing hot meat pies and sausage rolls, not to mention the steady procession of custard tarts and buttered Boston buns also ringing the till. There must have been a dozen or so people, but regardless of where they stood, Mrs Macklin always had the queue sussed; anyone who tried to jump it was rebuked and, often as not, bumped back a place.

Alan didn't speak as we shuffled our way up to the counter. When we got to the "Next!" position Mrs Macklin, a friend of my mother's, treated me to her especial charming smile and asked, loud enough for everyone in the place to hear, "So! Larry! How's the sweet sixteen birthday boy? Happy as?"

I heard the titters and I caught pink-faced Sharon's quick smirk. "Not 'til tomorrow," I mumbled, working hard at holding my own nicest smile.

"Well I hope you have a nice party and get lots of nice presents. I hear your uncle Jim is bringing old Bessie up for the day. That'll be nice."

I could have killed her. Half the town knew about the haircuts great-uncle Jim inflicted upon me and my brothers. Not even his two-bob bribes to practice his hobby (these days it would be called a fetish) compensated for the short back and sides and the dinky little wave he so carefully crafted. Even the farm kids who showed up at school with their basin cuts laughed at us. It wasn't funny.

Alan, the banker's son, snapped down a mint two-shilling piece. "Two sausage rolls with sauce, please," he said, bumping things back on track. "My shout for the birthday boy," he clarified, nodding at me, standing there doing a pretty good impersonation of a dummy.

There could not have been a more public place for Alan and me to be seen together. Then, icing on the cake, so to speak, as we left the shop — in comes "Oh Really" O'Reilly. And Alan, brazen as you like, holds the door for him.

The copper thanked him but winked at me.

So, the fat was in the fire.

We sat together on the town hall steps.

Alan pointed at the cheap box of a building that had recently filled the vacant lot left after the rubble of Scriber's Emporium had been finally cleared away. "Before my time," he said. "You remember it?"

"Watched it from up there," I nodded up the steps at

the hall's front terrace. "We all saw it," I added, "saw the whole thing."

"Good show?"

"Bloody ripper!"

"Your mate, Scott?" he asked, quick as a flash. "He see it?"

"Well ... no, I mean, not everybody used to go to the Wednesday night show. My father used to take me. War films and Westerns and, you know, all that stuff."

I could have added that Dad now preferred to put on his slippers, settle into his big armchair in front of the open fire and watch *Bonanza*, *Rawhide*, *Gunsmoke* and *Have Gun Will Travel*. But such details were too personal to share with someone like Alan Baker.

Lining himself up to take the first bite of his sausage roll, Alan remarked, almost to himself, "At least he can't blame me for that one."

Refusing his bait, I chomped off the first mouthful of my own feed. It had cooled to scoffable and that's what I did with it.

"I'm sorry you and Scottie got the cuts," he said. "Nothing I could do about it. You know, my father ... with his job and all, he was in an awkward position. I suppose you know there was trouble before ... with my sister?"

"Mad Marlene," I said, cool as you like. "Yeah. She decked your Mum. Everybody knows that."

If he was annoyed he didn't show it. "Actually," he drawled, a shade too archly, "there was a bit more to it than that. Even so, my father can't have another *awkward* thing. His job's all about reputation. Believe me, that fact of life has been drummed into me — the hard way, if you get my drift."

"So why stir things up? You had Scottie dobbed for looking in your locker. You could have copped it. We didn't take anything. But no! No, no ... THEN! Having already got us into trouble, you push everything along by putting that bunger in his locker. What the ...?"

"Aww what? Come off it!" He laughed in disbelief.

I took a big bite and munched like blazes, wondering whether this bloke was the brain-box he was supposed to be.

"You see," I said carefully, "I'll be asked about this conversation. What's to stop me just telling Sergeant Mac you admitted putting the thing in Scottie's locker? Even if you call me a liar, I reckon the good old Sarge will have enough doubts ... and, you know, mud sticks."

He tried to get ahead of me. "You can tell anyone whatever you bloody well like, you sneaky little bastard. I'd deny it until the cows came home and then I really would look for a way to get you two. Even if some shit stuck to me, believe me, things would only get a lot worse for Scott. Naw ... and to think I came here to say we ought to let things cool off."

"I'm listening."

"I don't think I can trust you."

"Even so," I wiped my fingers on the paper bag, "perhaps we should call a truce."

"A truce?"

"Call it a cease fire," I laughed. "With summer coming ... not the best time to be caught playing with matches."

I looked at him then. I looked him square in the face but saw nothing behind the mask. "So you reckon," he said, looking away, "Scottie did light that half-arsed fire at the prefab? Or try to light it."

"Doesn't matter what I think. We both know that's the general opinion."

"I dunno," he shrugged. "All I know is that it wasn't me. So, who else?"

"It wasn't Scottie. Could have been anyone."

"If you say so."

"I do say so."

He looked back at me. "Anyway ... a truce? A truce! What that's supposed to mean?"

"Don't be tiresome," I crooned my line as I had practised it. "You know what it fuckin' means."

His eyes widened and he snorted, "You make it sound like we're in cahoots!"

"No. Just calling a truce."

He stared at me in silence. I think he wanted to make me feel uncomfortable, but, honestly, to let you into a secret, I was mostly embarrassed — for him.

I smiled, beamed at him. He blinked and averted his eyes. Perhaps he was also embarrassed. He seemed to be absorbed by something in the midair distance. Finally, he stood and carefully brushed the small flakes of pastry from his jacket. "All right then. But I'll just say," his voice so low I could barely hear him, "no more shifty stuff. I'm telling you: Leave it alone!"

I couldn't resist. "But if it wasn't you and it wasn't Scottie? If there's someone else besides old Bernie what's-his-name ... I mean, what happens if there's another fire?"

"Scottie still gets the blame. Whatever you say about throwing mud, fact is, he's IT for now. And neither of you can change that. If he leaves it alone, I'll do the same. But if he comes after me again, it'll backfire on him. Tell him I said that. I mean it in a friendly way. And yes, like you say, a truce."

He left without another word.

"A *truce*?!"

"That's what he said."

"Ha!" Scottie's finger of exclamation shot skyward like a rocket on his rigid arm. "Ha!" he repeated, seemingly unable to find any better expletive to splutter his indignation.

119

"He said he was sorry we got the cuts, but he wants to let things cool off. He said he wants a cease fire."

"A *what*?!"

"A cease fire."

"Ha!" He stamped his foot.

"I think he's frightened his father will ..."

"Bastard!"

"... he said his father ..."

"What? His father! Ha! What's he gunna do? Complain to Porkie again? Go to the cops?"

"Something like that."

"As if that changes my ... my ... situation," he spluttered and spat.

"He sorta said that ..."

Scottie swallowed and hunched his shoulders. He seemed to suddenly withdraw into himself. "Thinks he's got it all figured out! This is bullshit."

"No, I ... I think he's fair dinkum."

Scottie cut me off with an impatient slice through the air of his open hand. "Bullshit! Bool-*shit!*" His narrowed eyes met and held mine. "And you believed him," he as good as sneered at me. "Are you supposed to take him an answer?"

"Don't think so."

He blinked a few times, paused on a breath and then nodded to the dawning of some inner satisfaction. "Good," he said through a tight smile. "Well, now, that's that then."

I believe that was the last time I saw Scottie smile.

V

The last fire was at the top corner of the Croquet Club green, near the Bakers' back fence. That was where Scottie burnt himself attempting to throw a Molotov cocktail. For a couple of days before they dug it up and replaced the damaged turf, you could see the extent of the splash of burning petrol and oil.

Regarding Molotov cocktails. As far as I can say, Scottie had never before had a go at making one. Like everybody, we'd seen the wartime pictures and read general descriptions in books and magazines; but, as in all things, the gap between theory and practice inevitably creates room for error. And with volatile substances that gap is especially tricky. Unforgiving. Things have to be done just so.

Naturally enough, *after* Scottie's accident, I made further studies as to the theory and practice of this matter. You must *fill* the bottle with fuel. Not with fuel *and* air. That tends to explode *in* the bottle. Your classic Molotov cocktail (invented by the Finns) works best when it delivers fuel and fire separately — together, but separately — so that they mix on impact. *Whumpa-whoosh!* Do not confuse a wick for a fuse. The wick doesn't even need to be a piece of whatever is used to stopper the bottle. It can be just a strip of kero-soaked cloth tied around the neck of a corked or screw-top bottle.

I don't know what happened. Scottie knew a thing or two about chemistry and the making of things, so you would think — Wouldn't you? — that he could have worked out those sorts of details. I don't know ... in the dark, in his excitement.

The whole thing was wrong. Carried away by what a huge joke he thought it would be, he didn't think it through. Even if he landed his bomb on the roof of the shed and burned the place to the ground, everything would have implicated him rather than Alan. The Arson Squad would have soon found the stitching in the sack.

At first, people didn't know what to think. It was far too shocking. Most of them had never encountered anything like it. Not in real life. They were deeply troubled by talk of Scottie's "malicious fixation" and related psycho-maniacal matters; troubled and confused because, really, they just didn't know what those secret turn of the mind words actually meant. What they understood was that all the fancy talk ultimately came down to the hard fact that the kid was mental, that he had gone round the bend.

Only on the second or third day did a few of our more reflective citizens wonder aloud about whether or not that ginger son of the bank manager was an entirely innocent party in the murky saga. Then it came out that the Sergeant had discovered Alan had been talking about a summer truce, "a ceasefire".

"A *what*?!" asked all and sundry.

Further bafflement and head scratching ensued.

In the end, the only certainties were that Scottie flipped out and the consequences were bloody awful. Between sips of afternoon tea during private conversations with like-minded souls, the people of the town opined that the poor boy had brought misfortune upon his own silly self. It was known he read a whole lot of nonsense, and that he and his drongo mate (yours truly) had fooled around with fireworks, but the kid himself wasn't offering any explanations and so everything remained in the realm of speculation.

It was the utter horror of Scottie's disfiguring injuries that led those lounge room conversations into the safer territory of pious but heartfelt expressions of pity for his poor mother. The woman looked a fright. Really, it was quite tragic. No other word for it.

Need I say that Sergeant McPherson came down on me like a ton of bricks. As did my mother and father and just about everybody else.

I defended myself. I'd been loyal to my friend and stubbornly insisted that was what mattered. Besides — it wasn't fair! — I felt bad enough about Scottie's accident without everybody loading extra guilt onto me.

I spent a fair bit of time staying with various relatives in different parts of Victoria.

It took a while, but on the surface at least, it blew over.

I guess a lot of people still wonder about those fires all those years ago. All I can say is that the trouble really started with the big fire that destroyed the classroom block. The Boom-TZAhSCH! one they eventually pinned on old Bernie Sumpter. Things were complicated by the smaller, follow-up fire at the demountable replacements a few weeks later. That was bad timing for Scottie. Bernie was locked up by then, but someone set those fires. Alan? Scottie? Did they do one each? As a sort of game? I can't say. Perhaps it was somebody else. Someone nobody suspected. Isn't that often the way of it? That "someone" under your very nose.

After all this time, how can anyone ever know? Private memories pale and fade. Public, collective memories are nebulous, shamelessly rewritten every decade or so. Knowledge erodes. Tracks are covered.

Scottie died a few years later. I only saw him the one time. I was taken to visit him in the hospital in Melbourne. Actually, strictly speaking, I didn't see him. He was all swaddled up. I don't think he had yet realised the extent of his injuries. We could not say much. With my parents and Mrs Scott in the room, it was pretty tense.

I never saw him again. We exchanged a few letters, but only for a year or so.

If he ever came to suspect anyone other than Alan, he apparently never said so. I believe he kept his mouth shut to the bitter end, when, as I like to think of it, he followed his trail of liquid light into another room.

Scottie might have been a bit cracked, as they all said, but I say he was still a good bloke. What happened was a bloody shame. A real pity. It was an accident. A tragedy. I know that word has been worked to death, but I still say Scottie's fate was tragic.

Alan Baker also disappeared from my life. I never spoke to and hardly ever saw him again. He was sent off to a posh boarding school in Melbourne. His father was transferred to Bairnsdale. A few years later I heard Alan had won a scholarship and was studying medicine at Melbourne University and, later still, that he had gone off to America to work for a big drug company. I recently searched for him on the internet, but couldn't find anyone to fit the bill. Supposing he's still alive, he's most likely retired by now. He probably has grandkids the same age as we were then.

And, let's face it, those kids most certainly will be up to their own kinds of mischief. After all, that's just part of growing up.

The Exercise Book

In cleaning out mother's house for the estate sale, I finally had to deal with the two cartons containing all my father thought fit to retain from his thirty-five years as a police officer. Mum had mentioned them a couple of times before she died, but I never got around to them. In truth, I forgot about them.

They were under a couple of blankets on top of the spare room wardrobe. Dad must have put them up there sometime between his retirement twenty years ago and his death nine years later. The packaging tape may have lifted, but you could still see they had been sealed and secured to deter casual examination.

They contained correspondence, photocopies of seven case files, crime scene photographs, Police Gazette notices, newspaper clippings, notebooks, two reams of foolscap paper and a certain amount of pilfered office supplies. There were also a few things that were either my father's personal possessions or, perhaps, items of material evidence he souvenired. I was most impressed by a well-made flick-knife, a very dangerous piece of work in the wrong hands. There was an old Dr Pat tobacco tin containing three deformed, spent 303 bullets and several small nuggets of gold — thrown together like that, such things do invite speculation. There were WWII medals and an army signaller's Morse handset, which probably belonged to my grandfather, who served in New Guinea. None of the accompanying documents referred to these things, so their provenance remains a mystery.

My father had been an orderly man, so the random jumble of private and official material surprised me. Thinking about it, I recalled once hearing Mum say he had lately been "busy sorting out his papers". My guess is that he got fed up with the task of culling and hastily tossed whatever he had saved into the two boxes with the intention of properly sorting it later, a time that never came.

"What we acquire needs us alive." Who was it said that?

How often have you heard someone, looking at an old photograph, wish so and so was still with us in order to tell us where and when the picture was taken, to put a name to a face? It is an all too common story. Indeed, it is the standard story. Some things have an inherent value (I sold those nuggets for a tidy sum), but most do not. Once the bird of memory has flown, meaning falls away. A loose feather in the wind, as someone said.

Dutifully, I worked my way through the stuff to trace Joseph Peter O'Reilly's career from his Victoria Police recruitment in 1961 until his retirement as Senior Sergeant in 1996. Dad was the quintessential country copper. Apart from temporary, relieving duties at the start of his career, before he married Mum, he was stationed in relatively quiet country towns — Kyneton, Warrnambool and Ararat — good places to raise a family. I do not remember Kyneton, where I was born, but I have very pleasant memories of growing up in the other places. Dad's last fifteen years were in Ballarat, where he and Mum then retired. I only had a couple of years there, finishing my secondary schooling before leaving home to attend university in Melbourne.

Dad did not talk about his work at home. As I grew

older I sometimes overheard a brief remark to my mother, or enough of a telephone conversation to realize something was "up" or, more seriously, "on", but there was never any detailed information. It was understood, such matters were not for domestic discussion. So most of those police files and notices retained by my father concerned matters of which I had never heard. The only link I could make, a reason for him making and holding copies of those documents, was that they all related to unsolved cases. As I said, there were seven of them. The more serious were two dealing with the activities of firebugs in Warrnambool and Ballarat. The rest were relatively minor cases of property damage; minor but reoccurring, persistent. Some on-line research allowed me to trace three of the suspects in those cases. They were all dead. Should the others still be alive they would be quite old. The Police should have retained the original files, so I intend to destroy my inherited copies.

Of most interest to me was an item I did not immediately fully appreciate. Among the various notebooks was an old school exercise book. Only when I was some way into reading through the writings it contained did I realise they were prospective notes and rough drafts for magazine articles. This was a side of my father of which I did not know. But the handwriting was definitely his and several of the stories were headed with his notion of a catchy title. He had also made notes to himself as to which magazines he thought may show an interest in his efforts.

I found no finished articles and no correspondence to or from magazine publishers. The potential markets my father nominated were those popular post-war magazines now entirely redundant and defunct. They included such titles as *Australasian Post, Pix, Wide World* and *Walkabout.* He had saved a few issues of *Wide World* and *Walkabout*. In the 1950s and early '60s such reading material could be found in many Australian homes. But then television eroded their place in the world before they were finally washed away by the internet. They contained short fictional and "true" stories illustrated with vivid drawings or stark photos. Salacious, gristly or notorious crime stories were regular fare. Some of those magazines were larded with cartoons and all were well padded by advertisements for briar pipes, binoculars, men's grooming products and Austin cars. Other content included crosswords, horoscopes and columns of jottings under such titles as "Titbits" or "Worth Knowing!". In later years, to hold their place in a shrinking market, there was a drift towards displaying real tits and bits, as we used to say.

I found no completed manuscript and, as far as I can discover, my father never submitted any of his compositions to the publications he had considered. Nothing, at least as far as I can discover, was ever published under his name.

The first twenty pages of the exercise book (together with an inserted loose note) were dedicated to the Kyneton fires affair. This was a case for which my father had not obtained a copy of the official record, although he had newspaper clippings about it, together with a couple of glossy, black and white, 8x10 crime scene photos. I believe my father thought what that murky business had in common with the other cases he hoarded was the glimpse it offered of a community stricken and damaged by suspicions and tension in the wash of unsolved crimes; of a community fearing it had fallen prey to one of its own.

As I said earlier, I was born in Kyneton, in the year after the fires. My mother once told my former wife I was conceived the night the town's bonfire was set alight.

Actually, it was because of my mother's interest that the Kyneton fires case was one of the few items of official business of which I did hear snippets as I was growing up. I think the fate of the Scott boy bothered my mother as much as it did my father.

As with the other cases my father hoarded, I sought information concerning the whereabouts or fate of those involved. Ronald Alexander Scott died in February 1974. He is buried in Springvale Lawn Cemetery. I don't know what became of his parents. There are a number of Alan Bakers of the right age around, but I cannot tie any of them to the bank manager's son in Kyneton in 1964. There is a Laurence Henry Morgan in Queensland, a successful property developer and tour operator at Caloundra.

So, for what it may be worth, I have transcribed and extracted the following material from my father's exercise book. This is what he wrote about the Kyneton fires. I give it without editorial interventions to improve style or impose structure on what were, plainly, rather random observations and thoughts over a number of years.

THE KYNETON FIRES (1964)
Notes by Senior Constable Joseph O'Reilly

There have been two fires at the high school. The first (six weeks ago) completely destroyed an entire block of classrooms. The second (week before last) damaged one of the prefabs sent up from Melb. as temporary classrooms while a new block is built on the site of the first fire. McP is in two minds. He suspected kids for the first fire, but Arson say it's linked to another fire they're investigating. But they don't rule out local kids for the second (prefab) fire. ~~Subsequent events~~

McP wants us to keep an eye on a few likely lads. The Headmaster's main suspect is a 15 y-o named <u>Ronald Scott</u>. Father a slaughterman — quite respectable — but the kid has a reputation for being a bit odd. Also interested in <u>Alan Baker</u> — bank manager's son. His family had trouble with a pregnant (father unknown) older sister who was rushed off to "boarding school". Scott is an only child & Baker is the only one at home. Both boys quite smart & have knowledge of chemicals. Also watching <u>Larry Morgan</u>, the Lands Dept Inspector's oldest boy. He is Scott's best mate and hanger-on. McP thinks he may spill something useful on Scott.

The fire that destroyed the classroom block was the biggest in the town since the Emporium was burnt down. Before my time. McP is certain that one was an insurance job. He and the assessors dragged out the investigation but couldn't stop the owner being paid out. The old rogue moved to Qld and McP ruled a line under the matter. Says it's someone else's problem but it still narks him.

Scott & Baker are said to be sworn enemies. No clear reason. Just don't like one another. Scott accuses Baker of setting the first fire. Says it was a time bomb! General opinion: the kid reads too much and has a vivid imagination.

I wonder if by calling them "enemies" we are missing a rivalry factor. Scott is known to be impulsive, but maybe that's just an extra dose of a growing boy's hi-jinx. He and his mate loiter behind the tennis courts perving on the girls — fairly normal. On the other hand, Baker is a loner. ~~There's something not~~ Loners should always be watched.

We suspect Scott for the prefab. Access & motive. Not so sure of Morgan, who also had access via the paddock behind the tennis courts. But in that night's infernal fog the pair of them could have walked there up the middle of the road!

Some bright wag thumb-tacked a Fire Prohibition Notice on the Station's front door last night. One of those canvas ones for nailing on trees & fence posts. Quite a few people must have seen it before McP opened up. Whoever did it won't be so game if McP gets his paws on them. He asked Tom W who had access to the Brigade's stock. Tom said they were waiting on a new supply and pointed out that it looked like it had already been in the weather and was probably one taken down by someone at the end of the last fire season. Could have come from anywhere. McP asked us "Who takes down official Fire Prohibition Notices?" and answered himself with "Bloody kids!"

I was right. Quite a few saw that Fire Notice before McP took it down. The whole town enjoying the joke. McP ropeable. Access this time was easier for the Baker boy. But it could have been anyone. Someone is laughing behind our backs.

<u>Theory and Practice of gathering of Evidence</u>
Sgt Douglas M. McPherson: "I never cease to be amazed at people's capacity to tell barefaced lies! Contrary to what happens on Perry bloody Mason — your confronted villain rarely breaks down and confesses. They just say they don't know what we're talking about and walk away. And, as we know, they <u>can</u> walk away!"

He's right. There are kids now who are not frightened of us. Make an accusation and they just sneer and demand we "prove it!" They <u>know</u> they can walk away!

Everybody knows Scott is a watched suspect, but the town wants more. They want to pick at the thing. They've all got theories. Annoying — but we can't disregard the apprehension. Instead of just ~~calling~~ describing what we are hearing around the town as gossip, McP said it is "a concoction of hearsay and leaping invention that only the mentally ill would take seriously." That was said privately, of course, to Terry and me. Our Sgt does have a clever turn of phrase. He's the sort of ~~fellow one can learn a lot from~~ officer from whom one can learn much.

He also said a ~~funny~~ witty thing the night of the prefab fire. After the brigade left we walked down through the school grounds to the playing fields, where the bank of fog was at its thickest. "So then, Dr Watson, what do you think? Is the Hound of the Baskervilles out there?" I cupped my hands and did my baying dog call to set off most of the hounds around the town. You've got to have a laugh sometimes.

<u>Mon, 28 Sept '64</u>
The three of us were having a cup of tea and a yarn in the office this afternoon when, out of the blue, Terry says he loathed (his word) the stench of beer and vomit after

a six o'clock swill. McP told Terry he'd let him into a little secret. The way he grinned I thought he was going to tell us he'd had the same aversion when he joined the force. I should have remembered — McP became a cop already toughened up by the army, New Guinea and so on. He said that if Terry really wanted to be "a proper copper" he best get to like the smell of beer, vomit & shit. "It's your bread and butter," he said. We all laughed, but Terry got the point — cops can't be squeamish and they can't afford to be seen to be squeamish.

A pony belonging to Silent Knight got out of its paddock behind the State Houses. It was on the road out to the Golf Course. Bill Hunt rounded it up and came in to tell us he thought someone deliberately let it out. Advised the Knight Bros to put a lock on their gate.

I came face to face with Ronald Scott's mother the other morning. She came out of Coles, putting her purchases in her bag and not looking where she was going. I stopped in my tracks to let her pass and she also stopped as she looked up. I smiled at her and she tried to do the same, but it came across more as a frown. She was startled and a bit confused. It only lasted a second, but I looked into her eyes and saw fear. She looked so defenceless I could not but feel sorry for her and her troubles. I didn't know what to say. She is still a good looking woman, but the strain of all that's going on is starting to show. She excused herself, stepped around me and hurried off along the street.

When Bern. S was caught over at Broadford, we were told it was 99% he was responsible for our classroom block fire. He continues to deny it but McP says Whelan says BS will definitely wear it. The estranged

133

wife told Arson a few unsavoury things they could threaten to pass on to Vice Sqd. McP pulled a face but didn't say anything. I once heard him describe a well-known member of Vice as being "as slippery as an eel". Something happened when he was serving in Port Melbourne and he's convinced that once Vice get their grubby hands on a case there's nothing left but lies. I agreed with him.

McP has taken to calling me "Dr Watson". Our private joke.

We were all out last night (8 Oct) until after midnight. Bert Williams reported someone skulking about the sheds and grounds behind the primary school the night before. Bert's an old Digger pushing 70 who wears thick glasses, so how he could have seen anything on a wet, dark night is a mystery to me. I said as much but McP said we can't afford to ignore it. He reasoned a show of vigilance would sit well with the town and give pause to anyone with mischief in mind. I can't help thinking that if our firebug couldn't succeed with a shoddy pine prefab, he's not likely to get far on a hundred-year old, solid bluestone building on a wet night. I admit the toilet blocks, cloak rooms and shelter sheds might be at risk, even if it has rained all week.

I don't mind foot patrols. You can take your time and relax. No doubt I'd feel different if I had bad feet. But mine are still in good shape. Old Cooney used to say you should make sure you have good boots and a good bed because you are in one or t'other all day. The station has a car and a couple of pushbikes but unless there's some hurry I prefer to walk, especially at night. You see and hear more on foot. What's better than being out under a full moon on a clear night? Especially in summer. Ask the lads who take the girls down to the river at the back of the gardens! But we can't be so relaxed and looking the other way now we suspect someone in the town of being up to no good. McP keeps telling us we'll need to be on our toes to catch this little bastard.

Last night I took the beat west of Mollison St and Terry had the east side of town. He got the high school & sale yards, I had the primary school, Marist Bros. & the Baker res (lights out 10.10 pm). The Sgt took the car round town, including parking for a spell on Boundary Rd to watch the Scott res. After the picture show he gave a pair of old chaps a lift home. It was quite cold and drizzling. I sat out one shower in the school shelter shed. The collars of these fancy new raincoats are too narrow and I got fairly soaked. Mary unhappy about the whole business. She waited up for me, reading by the fire after the TV finished. We had a nice warm cup of cocoa before bed.

At least we didn't have to be out in a fog like that one last month. I don't like the fogs here. A bit of mist is one thing, but sometimes the fogs here are so thick you can hardly see from one street light to the next. The fogs here also seem especially cold, chilling. You can't hear things properly either. Someone walking in front of you suddenly seems to be walking behind you. I've never seen any of those mysterious figures like they say they see in blizzards — someone going on ahead or following — but I got a terrible fright one night when an owl flew out of a tree in Ebden St as I walked underneath. ~~The delirium of the mist~~.

I won't call them nightmares, but I have had bad dreams about the fog. Always the same thing — three or four times now. It feels something like when you are delirious. It's not what you see, but what you sense. Mary says I don't groan or call out, but that dream usually seems to wake me.

<u>Weds, 14 Oct '64</u>: McP & Terry went into Wilson's today to supervise unpacking and storage of fireworks. All in order — locked in steel cabinets under stairs. Mrs Wilson notified we'd come by to check at night & make sure her place locked up. We wouldn't want it hit by the firebug. Terry said the old girl was all over the Sgt like a rash. Cream biscuits with the cuppa. She knows he could make it awkward for her because last year she definitely sold kids loose 3d bungers. Everything this year is to be sold in the manufacturers' packaging & there's to be no 3d bungers whatsoever. Terry saw the invoices and reckons the markup is at least 100%. Mrs W not permitted to sell any of her stock before next week, adults only, but she will then clear about <u>£300 in two weeks</u>. That's a big tin of biscuits.

The Sgt tells us extra men to be sent down from Bendigo for Kyneton Cup. People come from all over and reinforcements are required for general on-course policing. Hopefully, they also help prevent too many drunk-in-charge clowns getting onto the highway at the end of the day. There are at least 4 plainclothes men coming up from Melb to watch for known villains & protect the bookies — the only certain winners at any race meeting. Terry & I to man the Station, on standby in case someone's for the lock-up.

It'll be a busy week: Melb Cup on Tuesday; Kyneton Cup, Wed; then Market Day & Guy Fawkes on Thurs. The Lions are building a giant bonfire on the Show Grounds. McP and Tom Wedge are talking a lot & generally working one another up about the thing. Personally, I think our little firebug has been scared off & pulled his head in.

Spoke too soon.

Doug McP is rattled. We all are. Someone put a timed device into the bonfire and it went up in the early hours of 5 Nov. There is a level of expertise and cunning about this ... Hard to credit any kid in this town capable of putting together something so complicated and dangerous. Sumpter's accounted for. So, who? Someone local? Someone who came into town under cover of the race meeting? Is that what we are supposed to think? That's what Whelan thinks. He was obviously disappointed to learn all horses for the Cup meeting were stabled at the track. Nobody was at the Show Gds. The place was locked up.

Sgt and I searched there early in the night. No sign of anything untoward. He sent me home but then he sat alone in the grandstand in the wet and cold until near midnight. It had been a long day, but he stayed on duty. He was no sooner home and asleep than the fire siren woke him. I might have slept through it if Mary hadn't roused me.

Sgt paid the Scotts a visit in the small hours and found the kid at home, dry as a bone. He had not been out. But then we later found the device had been planted as much as a day beforehand.

I know we have to figure out the How, but I'd like to know the <u>Why?</u>

This morning (6 Nov) I had the task of collecting Jeff Scott from his place of work to be present as his residence was searched and his son questioned. He was really angry — cold anger — but he kept himself in check and cooperated fully. I could not fault his behavior and I'm starting to think his son may not be who we are looking for. Whelan & McP are keeping their views to themselves. ~~They're as mystified as the rest of us.~~ The evidence I found at the fire site is going to Melb with

Whelan. Not sure they'll find anything we can't work out for ourselves. Sgt on the TV last night.

Terry sent to door-knock all residences in streets adjoining Show Gds. Long day for him. McP gave him the blackest look when he reported that nobody saw anything. Caretaker confirms the main gate locked all day. But the culprit would have come in the back, across the paddock from the Commission Houses. After lights out, in the early hours, nobody would see a thing. Fortunately for Terry, he remembered to ask if any dogs had barked. Unfortunately for us, nobody noticed them if they did.

Terry asked what I thought about Alan Baker. Asked if Sgt would search his place. Told him he & Whelan had been there most of the afternoon. Nothing suspicious. Looked through some diaries — a lot of drivel, poetry etc. T asked what Whelan thought & I told him he was as mystified as the rest of us. "Must be the Viet Cong," T said. His idea of being funny. Advised him not to make jokes about this, especially to the Sgt.

We heard 3 or 4 carloads from Kyneton turned up at the Redesdale bonfire. Some drinking and skylarking but generally behaved themselves. The main news was that Johnny Humphries didn't deliver Sandra Bowman home until well past midnight. Mrs Bowman made the mistake of going out into the street and confronting Humphries, the neighbours heard all and now so does the town. Johnny said he got lost, took a wrong turn coming home. Time will tell whether young Sandra took her own wrong turn.

Arson say "the device" would have been easy enough to put together but they rarely see such things. Most of their cases are simply a matter of a tossed match. All of what we salvaged at Show Gds was readily available — even the clock could have been bought at Coles.

Fellows who usually only give me a passing nod now stop me in the street wanting to know what's what. We are under strict instructions not to discuss the case but I hint that the bonfire might have been done by someone from out of town. Nobody really believes that. "Why would an outsider bother?" I don't have an answer. Whelan is talking about a pyromaniac. In other words: a firebug who is <u>really</u> cracked. And damned cunning.

McP is annoyed by people pestering him about it. The Mayor bailed him up this afternoon. I didn't say so but I think you have to expect the curiosity and I actually find all the talk interesting. I also think it's a big part of basic police work — keeping an ear to the ground.

There are definitely tides and moods to a town's gossip. The mood was more apprehensive during the winter months, now anger dominates. This is of course primarily due to events, but I can't help feeling the seasons themselves colour the response.

One thing I can say: Ronald Scott is not doing himself any favours by continuing to spread stories about Alan Baker's bomb making abilities.

Just when we thought we had the measure of who's playing with who — at the pie shop I see Alan Baker openly associating with Ronald Scott's sidekick. Then we hear from Harry Morgan that Baker is asking Scott for a "truce"! If they are all so innocent of the Show Gds fire, what is such talk supposed to be about? Are they making fun of us? It is a question.

There are too many questions.

In the Bible the lake of fire and brimstone is the place of the <u>second</u> death. For Ronald Scott it was nearly death in the <u>first</u> place. He will live, but his burns are fearsome and are perhaps something worse than death for him.

I have been too busy (taking statements, typing reports and generally chasing about) to have time for my own notes. I'll go over the files later and try to fill in the gaps.

Harry Haller ran up the street to wake Doc Connell and then came around to get the Sgt. They wrapped the boy in a blanket. The Doc had him taken up to the hospital and immediately ordered an ambulance to take him to Melbourne. Gave him a shot of morphine and a sedative. Gave himself and us a shot of brandy.

McP went to tell the parents himself. Drove them up to our hospital. Told me the mother was calm and the father bawling. Not what we expected. Mrs Scott went down to Melb. in the ambulance with Doc Connell. Jeff Scott taken down by the abattoirs manager following in his car. McP went down in the morning to talk to Whelan and to see what he could get from the Scotts — which was nothing. Too soon, he said. Too late, I think.

It fell to me to talk to Baker. He's frightened. Scared out of his wits. Not making a lot of sense and denying everything. Insists the talk of "a truce" came from Scott and Morgan. Says Morgan's not what he seems. Who do you believe? We'll have to talk to him again. Took some photos at Croquet Club. A bad show all round.

Baker's mother has taken him off to the city and Baker Snr tells us his son will only be available for questioning in the presence of a lawyer. Says he's already had the lawyer contact the Arson Squad to arrange an interview in Melb. More or less out of our hands.

<u>1965</u>

A quiet New Year. A lot of families away for the school holidays. This year people are keener than usual to get away for a while. I'm looking forward to it myself. Mary & I have a couple of weeks off in Feb after school goes back. We'll visit our families and have a week to ourselves at Ocean Grove. Once school holidays are out of the way you can get a decent place at a reasonable price. Doug McP to take his annual leave first two weeks of March. Russ Samson will come up from Woodend for any Court work, but I'll be in charge of the Station's day-to-day. A little extra in the pay packet for the "Acting".

Weather remarkably cool for time of year. The papers say it's sweltering in Perth so it'll warm up here next week, but so far so good as far as bushfires are concerned.

Trouble-makers all have their heads down or have cleared out. Morgan sent off to an uncle in Ballarat for summer holidays. Baker gone — enrolled Melbourne Grammar. McP says the father seeking an urgent transfer. Mustn't speculate, but there is definitely something not right, out of kilter in that family.

Irene Scott stayed in Melb to be near her son. Mary heard she will not return and that the father is planning to sell up and join her. Everybody feels very sorry for them, but it's obviously the best thing for all concerned that they leave this place.

Nothing heard from Whelan or anyone else at Arson. They don't seem to be interested.

Mary was already certain anyway, but Doc Connell has made it official — due mid-August. ~~Great Expectations!~~ Like everybody else Mary is unsettled by what happened to the Scott boy. The more one thinks about it, the worse it gets. I know she is strong and that she has the certainty of her faith, but I must not let such a bad business cloud her anticipation of being a mother. A week at the beach with a couple of good books will do us both good.

I quite like the new priest. He's up-to-date, seen a bit of life, and keeps an eye out for problem kids. People like him can nip trouble in the bud and save us a lot of strife later on. We had a long talk one day last week about what he calls the "problem of evil". I told him I believed something wicked had passed amongst us last year and that I was not sure it would not return. I could see he took me seriously. Mary and I had not been attending Mass as regularly as we should, but we are now in a good routine.

Drove past the Lands Dept depot late yesterday and saw Harry Morgan assisted by his son loading a bag of carrots into a cement mixer — the pair of them wearing overalls and rubber gloves! I didn't stop but I later asked McP about the correctness of Morgan involving his son in the handling of restricted substances — i.e. 1080 poison. Said I wondered what else was in the Lands Dept shed and who has access. McP more or less shrugged it off by saying he'd have a word. But I reckon that'll be as far as it'll go. Perhaps I should have reminded him there are a lot of guns and ammo in the Morgan household.

Nobody ever talked, so we still don't know what Morgan Jnr had to do with that nasty business last year. I think he gets away with playing the fool a little too easily. His parents need to clip his wings. Somewhere along the way he has picked up the nickname "Whoosh". Nobody knows why. "Something he says a lot." It might be to do with the show-off, reckless way he rides his bike. Since Ronald Scott's exit Morgan is running with a different lot. They hang around down the back of the gardens, smoking & drinking. Someone's selling them plonk. We have a good idea who. Only a matter of time before we catch them. Now that National Service is back you'd hope cocky little hooligans like Morgan will eventually be knocked into line by the Army. Trouble is, we have to deal with them until they're 20.

Whoosh? You could write a book about country town nick-names. People can live most of their lives beside one another in these places without knowing a person's real name until it's in the death notices. Some are obvious. Like "Porky" Veal. "Talkie" Bell. Russell Montgomery, the plumber, has a long neck and is known as "Goose". And it suits — he is a goose. There's a girl here the lads call "Spanner" because they reckon she tightens their nuts. Mostly wishful thinking I'd say, but where there's smoke there's usually fire and I daresay one or two of them reckon they're on a promise. She's 16 and looks like butter wouldn't melt in her mouth but I told young Terry to never ever let himself be caught alone with her.

As expected, we finally nabbed three underage drinkers under the bridge. They had been supplied with two bottles of cheap port by Kevin Murphy (21). Stuart Reardon, David White and Kenneth Thorpe, all aged 16 and all classmates of Morgan. I am sure he was there. But we did not catch him. He didn't come out my side and Terry will be indignant if I insist he wasn't quick enough. Too bad. McP's comment: "So, the dog got wind of the rabbit but he didn't actually <u>see</u> the rabbit." Of course, the mates are not about to tell tales on one of their own.

I put in for Warrnambool. By the sea for me.

143

[Loose sheet]
12 May '67
Talked to Doug McPherson at the Drug Conference. Told me he'll get Senior later this year and has been advised to apply for Bendigo. He & Helen pleased with promotion although not looking forward to the move. But if you want promotion, you have to be ready to move.

Speaking of moves and promotion, he told me Harry Morgan was now a Snr Inspector & already transferred to Bendigo! Small world! Doug was laughing as he told me, but also shaking his head. "Trouble runs in that family," he said. Harry's second boy "borrowed" one of his old man's 22s and went after rabbits out towards the Golf Course. Result: lawyer from Melbourne, Club visitor, shot in the hand as he raised his club to tee off on the 16th. "You can f-ing imagine what Connell had to say about that," he said, still shaking his head but not laughing. There were questions asked in Melb. & Doug had to come down hard on Harry. He persuaded him to hand in a few of his guns. What was never explained was where the kid obtained the ammo. Doug reckons he got it from some of Larry's mates, but he couldn't prove it. Everybody just flatly denied any knowledge of anything. Doug gave me a funny look and said, "Remember, nobody confesses." He told me Larry had won a scholarship and gone to uni. "Not as silly as he looked," he said. Then, after a moment, he added, "He knew more than we thought he did, didn't he?" I said I thought so, too.

[Loose sheet]
7 March 1979
I saw Laurence Henry Morgan yesterday morning in the main street of Ballarat. I recognized him straightaway, even though he has long hair and is now about 30. First time I've seen him since Kyneton. I had to go down to

Ballarat for a meeting and ducked out at lunch-time to pick up a thing for Mary. I was crossing near the Boer War memorial and he was coming down from the Town Hall. I wasn't in uniform but I'm sure he spotted me. He looked the other way and marched off down the hill towards Bridge Street. I wish I'd had the time to follow and put the breeze up him. I had a quick look in the local phonebook, but couldn't see him. Visiting, perhaps. I later remembered he used to have relatives in or around Ballarat, so when I got home I dug out this old notebook and confirmed that detail. Uncle & aunt, unnamed. By the Govt Gazette I see old Harry is still with the Lands Dept, a Snr Inspector at Head Office. Finally got the promotion. Doug McP told me years ago about Harry's promising career having stalled after he got too stubbornly officious with a pig farmer who happened to be a brother-in-law of the Premier of the day. A Premier who was in the job for many years and who had a long memory. That was while Harry was down in the Western District, before he was shifted sideways to Kyneton.

I thought about phoning Doug, but I hear he's not too good, fading pretty fast. It's too late to trouble him with this old mess. It was Doug who phoned me from Traralgon five or six years ago to let me know Ronald Scott had ended his misery and that the parents had taken up a small place growing fruit and vegies somewhere up the coast near the Qld border. I guess they just wanted to get away from everything down here.

Afterword

Howard Willis is said to have described the interlocking stories of *Playing with Mischief* as "an exercise in smoke and mirrors". I say "said to have described" because, as with much to do with that secretive man, little can be directly attributed. Even so, the phrase is apt.

Along with real smoke, of which there is plenty, the stories are infused with a figurative smoke that obscures who is responsible for what. It is smoke that is, too, a whiff of the infernal. As to mirrors, consider the manner in which the diverse perspectives of these stories reflect back through one another. And then, beyond such obvious references, we should consider fiction's overarching artifice, in which Willis saw an affinity to the legerdemain of fairground magicians, the archetypical practitioners of smoke and mirrors.

Playing with Mischief (the title itself suggests an alternative: *Playing with Fire*) is also an exercise in stylistic variation. The paired novellas, *Mischief* and *The Fires*, third and first person narratives respectively, are bookended by the shorter pieces, *Invocation* and *The Exercise Book*, distinctly at opposite ends of the stylistic spectrum. These different, to some extent contending voices enhance the basic mirroring effect between the competing narratives. Or, to shift the metaphor, they create a space in which whispered implications echo.

Critics may argue the work's struggle to counter narrative indeterminacy with structural cohesion, and the novel's somewhat artificial structure, leaves little room for a clear authorial voice to emerge. Attentive readers, however, will discern the sly asides, the knowing nods and winks that characterize Willis's voice.

The osmosis by which the roots of reality nourish the flowers of fiction is always unclear, ambiguous, but of *Playing with Mischief* we may state a few plain facts. Much of the book's settings are derived from the author's childhood in the Victorian town of Kyneton, or from his adolescence in the city of Ballarat. Some of the characters are, in varying degrees, glosses of people he knew in those places: the teachers are "drawn from life"; his father really was a Lands Department Inspector. And while the novel's central dramatic imperative, the series of mysterious fires in and around Kyneton, is almost entirely fictitious, the burning down of the furniture store in the main street is a matter of historical record.

On the other hand, we know Willis moved to Ballarat at the end of 1963, when he was fifteen. He was not living in Kyneton in 1964, the year in which he ostentatiously sets *The Fires*. By presenting *Mischief*, the chronologically later (1965) Ballarat story, before *The Fires*, the Kyneton story, Willis was apparently seeking to cloud an autobiographical reading of his fiction. In proleptically hinting at something his reader does not come to until much later in the book, and then only by way of vicarious suspicion, he obscures cause and effect. The plot takes some time to come into focus. By the time the reader realizes the narrative sequence is unreliable there is a claustrophobic unease.

That uncertainty is given form, so to speak, by the nocturnal fog in which the Kyneton police seek to distinguish between real and imagined. But as the stories brush against each other a trail is glimpsed in the undergrowth of the night. Even though time and daylight make it clear Larry "Whoosh" Morgan could not have been responsible for all of the fires, suspicion settles on that self-proclaimed "gormless" narrator of *The Fires*. The reader, following the lead of Constable O'Reilly, senses rather than sees the seat of the fire. As in a book Willis admired, Randolph Stow's *The Suburbs of Hell*, the villain hides in open sight.

The discrepancy between how characters are openly presented and what the writer may otherwise reveal was at the centre of Willis's thoughts on fiction. In broad terms, it was the difference between how we depict ourselves and the way others see us. That line of thought goes to explain the strength of his disappointment at the reception of his *What Comrade Oldie Knew*. Despite that novel's insistence that we cannot trust appearances — indeed, we cannot even trust the ground beneath our feet — many readers apparently expected and therefore saw in it little more than rough autobiography. I believe it was to counter such a reading of *Playing with Mischief* that Willis paid so much attention to its structure. And it was not lost on him that a novel about deception was given further depth by employing "smoke and mirrors".

Willis's readiness to play with narrative structure was reinforced by his chronic disenchantment with contemporary Western literary culture, in which he saw "writers replacing writing". Always ready to recognize and laud genuine talent, he nonetheless regarded the tediously polished conformity of what he termed "writing school product" and its associated falderal as a blight on the literature of the English-speaking world.

His eccentric belief was that educational institutions best serve the public good by encouraging people to read rather than fostering vain literary ambitions.

Although he may have overtly rejected any notion of literature predicated on the marketed persona of an author, in effect Willis still subscribed to an alternative, contradictory view of the writer as hero. He sought the works of stylistic innovators; works of intelligence in which the forms and structures were outside those of the standard chapter-a-day novel or magazine length short story. Should such writers be astute observers questioning social mores, writers perhaps even shunned and ridiculed by their contemporaries, so much the better. He saw infamy as a far more accurate measure of literary worth than confected fame.

Describing himself as "a heavy reader", Willis was drawn to the literatures (and films) of other cultures, arguing that not only did the majority of literature first appear in languages other than English, but that the time entailed in bringing "foreign" writings to translation went a long way towards winnowing out the dross. He was, frankly, somewhat snobbish in his arcane, esoteric tastes. It was not surprising that he was annoyed when the cultural and literary references, with which he rather pretentiously peppered *Comrade Oldie*, were passed over, unnoticed or misunderstood. It may have been naïve of Willis to expect readers to find out about, and perhaps even watch, Georges Franju's 1963 film, *Judex*, a work concerned with masks and disguises, but he clearly gave and underlined the reference.

He read books from France, Italy, Spanish America and Japan, but his lifelong fascination was with eastern Europe, where the turbulence of falling empires and revolutions pushed boundaries and churned to the surface previously ignored or suppressed works.

While acknowledging the importance and bravery of openly dissident works, it was the oblique approach, the delicate balance of laughter through tears and the muted (but in plain view) sense of the absurd found in novels like Andrei Platonov's *The Foundation Pit* or Ludvik Vaculik's *The Guinea Pigs* that really engaged Willis. He renewed his study of Russian in order to better understand Platonov's subtle subversion of official language and took pride that during a visit to Moscow in 2013 he laid flowers on that writer's grave; *Comrade Oldie*, too, contained a few metaphorical flowers to Mikhail Bulgakov's *The Master and Margarita*.

The innovative traditions and intellectual milieu of European literature may have influenced the configuration of *Playing with Mischief*, but the story takes its tone from the raw helter-skelter of small town life in the antipodean backblocks. For this we should look to Ronald Hugh Morrieson's *The Scarecrow*, a book with which Willis, having lived in New Zealand during the 1970s, was familiar. He maintained that work's opening line was in itself sufficient to secure the novel's high place.

Willis's decade-long residence in Auckland produced no published fiction. His only publication was *Bad Blood*, a detailed account of the Stanley Graham shootings and manhunt on the South Island during WWII. The success of that book and the film based upon it determined that Willis was thereafter catalogued as a writer of non-fiction.

He returned to Australia in early 1980. After a couple of years in rural Tasmania he and his family moved to Perth, Western Australia. He continued to write and a few short stories appeared in small journals; most of his manuscripts were consigned to either the bottom draw or the stove. In the mid to late 1980s, he told various people he was working on a novel about post-war Darwin. It is not clear whether or not he destroyed that work, but it does seem to have been lost. No doubt due to his own obscurity, lost and late discovered masterpieces were of persistent and growing interest to Willis. He visited Gogol's house in Moscow and looked into the fireplace where Part Two of *Dead Souls* was burned. He wrote a magazine article about Bruno Schulz's lost work, *The Messiah*.

During the 1990s, in conjunction with his archival research for anthropologists and archaeologists working on native title cases, Willis was increasingly absorbed by Australian colonial history. This led to the transcription and annotation of various Western Australian exploration journals. The items that were published were all works he undertook in concert with others; the major work he did on his own (comprehensively annotating the 1865 Journal of Robert John Sholl) never saw the light of day.

It was during that period, when I took issue with one of his caustic book reviews, that we established a correspondence. My residency in Melbourne was for only one year (1996) and I did not have the opportunity to visit Perth, so although we spoke on the phone several times, we never met. He once told me he did not enjoy "the buffoonery of socializing". His letters, intermittent but always entertaining, continued for several years after I returned to Europe.

In the winter of 1998 Willis's youngest son, aged 19, was killed in a traffic accident. Without being able to explain it beyond saying he "seemed to have just lost interest", the writer read little or no fiction for most of the following decade. In the middle of those years he and his wife were forced out of their inner-suburban public housing. With the assistance of a modest inheritance, it took them fourteen years to discharge their mortgages on the small house they bought in Perth's northern suburbs. As depicted in *What Comrade Oldie Knew*, he was not at ease there. Afflicted by noisy neighbors and their constant renovations, he was often distracted and irritable.

Although willing, when asked, to provide editorial advice to others, he rarely sought opinions of his own work. He considered writing to be a private undertaking, preferring to work alone. Writing is certainly therapeutic, but the essential interaction is the underground one between the writer and his work. Writing as an excuse for a group therapy, talking cure rarely leaves anything of any enduring consequence.

Besides, he did not suffer fools gladly and, with a strong belief in rational thought, was ever-ready to argue. It is a pity, but it has to be said, his manner of discourse often seemed opinionated, even arrogant. He had a gift for antagonism. More than once in his later years he ruefully remarked that he had fought with everyone he knew. His ready admission that he was mostly at fault did not disguise or ameliorate his perplexed regret at that situation.

He was further aggravated by declining health. In late 2006 he was diagnosed with hepatitis C, which he said was given to him by a malicious sprite, but was probably contracted during a series of back surgeries and associated procedures in the mid to late 1980s. This portent of mortality seems to have sparked a renewed interest in the value and uses of fiction. It eventually resulted in *Comrade Oldie*.

In late 2015 I heard from a mutual acquaintance that, following unsuccessful drug treatment for the virus, he required emergency heart surgery. That experience further intensified his study and practice of fiction. Having swallowed his disappointment over the "applied recollections" of *Comrade Oldie* being largely misunderstood by readers confused by the links between memoir and fiction, he ventured deeper into the process by taking *Mischief*, a novella he had written some years before, and using it as a foundation to build the larger work of *Playing with Mischief*.

In early 2019 Willis undertook a further course of anti-viral drugs. This time the exhausting three-month regime finally rid him of hepatitis C. The disease, however, had taken its toll. Calling being cleared of the virus a "recovery" was, he said, akin to using the same term for the amputation of a foot to stop gangrene — damage, beyond repair, had been done. Hindered by forgetfulness and mental fog attributed to cirrhosis and incipient Alzheimer's, Willis found it difficult to make progress with his last work (working title: *Desiderium*), a convoluted narrative involving twins, doubles, doppelgangers, shadows and the memory of ghosts.

Cared for by his wife, he has lapsed into silence.

— Josephine Tey
Mallorca, 2020